THE EFFIE ENIGMA

THE MOTHERLESS MOTHERS

BY

ALUN BUFFRY

ADULT SCIENCE FICTION

THE EFFIE ENIGMA

THE MOTHERLESS MOTHERS

BY

ALUN BUFFRY

Published by ABeFree Publishing: 2019
ISBN 978 099 32107 9 2

Acknowledgements and Accreditations.
With thanks to John Adam, Melissa Dawson, Brian Clark, Steve Land, Mara Jolin, Lisa McKenna and Matteo Trisoglio for help with the text and to
Matt Maguire <info@candescentpress.co.uk> for the cover.
Thanks to Jacqui Malkin for the sketches.
Thanks to Wikipedia for the information.

BY THE SAME AUTHOR

FROM DOT TO CLEOPATRA, A CONCISE HISTORY OF
ANCIENT EGYPT
ISBN 1-872914-09-8 (Frontier Publishing, Windetts,
Kirstead, Norfolk, NR15 1BR, UK)
http://buffry.org.uk/fromdot.html

DAMAGE AND HUMANITY IN CUSTODY
ISBN 978-1-533-0262-2-4 (ABeFree Publishing)

OUT OF JOINT - 20 YEARS OF CAMPAIGNING FOR
CANNABIS
ISBN 978-1-508-4202-1-1 (ABeFree Publishing)
http://www.buffry.org.uk/outofjoint.html

ALL ABOUT MY HAT - THE HIPPY TRAIL 1972
ISBN 978-0-9932107-1-6 (ABeFree Publishing)
http://www.buffry.org.uk/allaboutmyhat.html

TIME FOR CANNABIS: THE PRISON YEARS
ISBN 978-0-9932107-6-1 (ABeFree Publishing)
http://www.buffry.org.uk/timeforcannabis.html

MYHAT IN EGYPT: THROUGH THE EYES OF A GOD
ISBN 978-0-9932107-7-8 (ABeFree Publishing)

All available at AMAZON and through good bookshops.

"LSD is just a tool to turn us into what we are supposed to be": Albert Hofmann.

"We choose to go to the moon in this decade and do the other things, not because they are easy, but because they are hard...": John F Kennedy.

SMILE: SM (Space Migration) + I^2 (intelligence increase) + LE (Life extension): Timothy Leary.

"I'm talking about sending ultimately tens of thousands, eventually millions of people to Mars and then going out there and exploring the stars.": Elon Musk.

"The first ultra intelligent machine is the last invention that man need ever make, provided that the machine is docile enough to tell us how to keep it under control." Irving John Good

"Those that control the future also control the past," Effie.

Translated from Several Old Earth Languages.

Connect 2121

Agent ZX (Zedex) had mixed feelings about being called to the Connect HQ. On the one hand, it meant endless hours scanning through news reports, watching old news films and scratching away at connections. On the more positive side, an opportunity to meet his latest crush, Agent QT, whom he called Cutie, from the Far East Sector of Connect. They had communicated virtually several times, but the thought of meeting Cutie in the flesh gave him goose pimples.

In the old days they used to call this day Saint Valentine's Day.

But, thought Zedex, what chance do I have? Cutie is an attractive young man, just about 22 years of age, with olive skin, visible muscles and long blond hair.

Zedex himself was probably, he thought, more of a father figure than a potential flesh-on-flesh lover. Now 98-years-old, rotund, balding, he still wore the old-fashion spectacles. He had never been comfortable with instant vision surgery that most partook of. All they had in common was that they were both investigating Crisis Connections and had both previously been with the military. Anyway, current events that were bringing them together were serious and they would have to focus.

But, remembered Zedex, Cutie will only have seen perfected image projection of him and vice versa. To Cutie, Zedex would have appeared forty years younger, several kilos lighter and with a full head of hair. And Zedex knew nothing about how Cutie actually looked in the flesh. This first meeting could well be a make-or-break.

Earlier that day, Zedex had been called to the HQ after four more deaths, this time all scientists all connected with Project Outreach. At the same time, there had been a failed attempt on the life of Professor John Sullivan, the creator of the portable wormhole in time.   Certainly this leaned towards the conspiracy theory.

So Zedex had taken an auto-hover car which enabled him to quickly catch up with the paperwork. Nowadays, few people moved about the city other than in auto-hovers which were remarkably safe. Fewer people actually travelled about the city than previously. What with food parcels delivered to your door, virtual teaching through the PLATO programme, the Planetary Tuition Optimisation scheme that brought almost identical tuition schedules into almost every home and put an end to the "school run" traffic chaos that Zedex had grown up with.

Zedex had received his instructions and a minimum amount of information via his retinal-link. Despite the safety record of auto-hovers, all four scientists, two men and two women, had died as a result of hover-car accidents. The chances of that being simple coincidence was indeed slim.

Connect was officially established way back in 2021, two years even before Zedex had been born (of course he was not called ZX back then) to investigate apparent connections between various historical events seriously retarding progress on Project Outreach, the building of the A.I.-controlled Mother-ships that would eventually enable distant planets to become human colonies, literally billions of years and even light-years from Earth. A.I. and robotics, cryogenics and space exploration itself were progressing comfortably but these events, whether connected or not, were slowing the project down to the point where earth's own problems could bring a halt to the project completely.

Zedex had entered Connect in 2098 and had been working virtually with Cutie for several years now and had listed incidents that had caused the delays in or seemed to have tried to delay project Outreach.

Until now it had appeared that it was merely a conspiracy theory that there existed a well-hidden long-term project to delay or stop Outreach. It had not officially been taken very seriously and Zedex's work was hardly a workload It was only now, with the sudden death of four essential scientists, that the newly appointed World President had prioritised the Connect project. The recent discovery of how humans and possibly others could use portable wormholes and the possibility of travelling through time introduced an entirely new line of investigation. It may become possible for people to travel to the past and make dangerous changes, cause all sorts of paradoxes; or even to the future. The possible assassination of the man at the leading edge in that technology, Professor John Sullivan, increased the likelihood that there was a connection between assassins over the decades and now there was news that Sullivan's suspected assassin had been "examined" and apparently the assassin thought he was indeed from the future and on a mission.

Cutie turned up with FE, pronounced Effy, his assistant, a gorgeous, shapely, young, woman with long flowing red hair and a big smile. She was a fit and bouncy girl of about 21 years of age and Zedex felt an immediate attraction to her. She was one of the elite super-IQ people that had been selected for this task. From the start Zedex saw her as the flirty type and thought she probably had a broad sense of humour. She smiled when she spoke or whenever Zedex looked at her directly. He saw that QT carried a case of electro-files.

Zedex did not feel ready. He had meant to don a wig and clean himself up a bit. Nowadays, people seldom met in the flesh. QT walked in, full of confidence and frowning, looking spectacular in Zedex's eyes.

QT was quite slender and tall but clearly muscular. His long blond hair was tied back in a pony tail. He had the start of a beard growth. He looked very serious. The sort of young man that seemed to find it hard to smile.

Zedex knew that, like himself, FE and QT were selected from amongst the most intelligent and successful people on the planet, suitable for Pure Information cloning to send out to colonise the galaxy through Project Outreach.

Zedez thought that QT and FE were like an ill-suited couple.

They clasped and shook hands as in the old days. Zedex wanted to hug him but that definitely wasn't on.

Zedex wanted to spend some time chatting, flirting, with either Cutie or Effy, or both, he didn't care. Just being with them and chatting with them would be such a unique and deeply personal memorable experience. Sex was desirable to Zedex although he thought it would be out of the question. Briefly he imagined himself in bed with both of them.

Zedex had prepared his introductory speech to explain to them what was the purpose of this meeting-in-the flesh.

Instead though, Effy stood up and began talking, reviewing the short history of the Connect project. She wanted them to study the links that the conspiracy theorists had pointed to.

The first event, said Effy, that they had known of was the assassination attempts on Albert Hofmann, who had discovered and synthesised LSD, Lysergic Acid Diethylamide, way back in 1928. At that time, the military was looking for drug weapons and in fact it was the US military that first conducted large scale tests using LSD on its' personnel in the 1960's.

Hofmann was born in 1906 in Baden, Old Switzerland, as it was known now, and had taken up his career in chemistry at the University of Zurich, finishing it in 1929. Hofmann provided insight during a speech he delivered to the 1996 Worlds of Consciousness Conference in Heidelberg, Old Germany: *"One often asks oneself what roles planning and chance play in the realization of the most important events in our lives."* Hofmann, had lived for over 100 years, not so common in those days, so it was quite possible that he became involved with the secret works of *Outreach*.

Many people thought that it was the consumption of LSD that had opened the minds of so many others also either involved in Outreach or involved in some of the steps and thought processes that had led to it.

Timothy Leary, the 'Acid-Guru' of the 1960's, was another. There had been assassination attempts against him too.

Other failed attempts were made against Steve Jobs and Bill Gates, the early computer entrepreneurs, who had also been reported as Acid users. The assassins had more success killing John F Kennedy in 1963, after his enthusiastic approach to space travel and putting man on the Moon.

Other major incidents that delayed Outreach considerably, were the Apollo 1 fire in 1968, the Challenger Space Shuttle that killed seven people in 1986 and the destruction of Connect Offices in the Twin Towers attacks in 2001.

Zedex was convinced that this series of events was down to a very secret organisation dedicated to stopping Outreach ever happening. So was Cutie. Effy said that she was unsure as often events that appeared to be connected were not.

Yet there was no hard evidence. The few culprits that had survived and been arrested and questioned, had several things in common. None of them had any sort of record, criminal or governmental; they had no fingerprints and there were no dental records, even though they all had, mysteriously, very bad teeth. They wore no masks but there were no photographs on file, anywhere: no health records, no records on birth or education or employment and the only words any of them had uttered were "outreach outrage".

Zedex and Cutie now had the job of crystallising probabilities into certainties, of making connections and making them real. They looked at screens, ran analytical and predictive routines, and spent several hours in isolation tanks after consuming micro-doses of Acid to expand their thought processes. They had to consider alternative realities, parallel universes and even time travel itself, and that would indeed be hard if sitting in a room looking at screens, and, Zedex thought, impossible for him to concentrate whilst sharing space with Cutie.

Cutie suggested that they "Get down to business right quick."

Dismissing the possible double-meaning, Zedex switched on the virtual screen which showed recent photographs of the four dead scientists. By pointing at a pic, they could read, or have read to them, short or longer biographies: it was amazing just how much data was held on almost everyone on the planet, and some off it!

After they finished reading each short bio, without planting too many preconceptions about Connections, the first step would be to use the A.I. to suggest them.

There were a great many of them, far more than either Agent would have imagined. A.I suggested Hofmann, Einstein, Tesla, Leary, Kennedy, Jobs, Musk and Sullivan as well as about twenty others in a secondary list. They would have to go through them one at a time, which would take days. Information came from official records, popular and alternative press reports, diaries and notebooks and even conspiracy theorists. Most of it was indeed public knowledge, unlike the conspiracy itself, which was hidden in the open. Instead of officially investigating the claims of the conspiracy theorists, successive governments had officially dismissed it all. They hadn't though. They had set up Connect instead.

Effy stood up saying that she had with her and would read througha series of reports on characters, events and information that was deemed connected to Operation Outreach and attempts at sabotaging it.

She read the reports aloud from her display pad.

ALBERT EINSTEIN: REPORT

Although there was no evidence of any attempts at assassinating Einstein or interfering in any way with his work, he is included here as possibly the earliest scientist that was essential to Project Outreach: but for his Special Theory of Relativity and his General Theory of Relativity, which predicted curves in space-time and worm holes, it was possible that the Project would never have been started.

Einstein had left his native Old Germany in order to avoid being drafted into the German military: he was already a pacifist.

After graduating, Einstein had been unable to secure an academic position and took employment in the Berne Patent Office. In 1903 he married Mileva Marić, December 29th 1875 to August 4th 1948, sometimes called Mileva Marić – Einstein or Mileva Marić-Ajnštajn, a Serbian mathematician. She was the only woman among Einstein's fellow students at the Zurich Polytechnic and was the second woman to finish a full program of study at the Department of Mathematics and Physics. Marić and Einstein were lovers and had a daughter Liesel in 1902 whose fate is unknown. They later had two sons, Hans Albert and Eduard.

In 1905, Einstein produced four academic papers:

1. Question what is Light?

2. Postulating the existence of atoms with calculations on size.

3. On the interchangeability of matter and energy that is $E = MC^2$.

4. The Special Theory of Relativity.

Einstein himself had written that "A storm rose in my mind" whilst he rode on a Berne city bus and looked at the City Clock. He had realised that space and time were one and the same.

There was not a good reaction until his paper was published by Max Planck later in 1905.

In 1907, Einstein published a new paper on Special Relativity theory, saying that his theory only applied to objects in one direction at constant speed and stated the need to apply the theory to everything, including gravity and to expand it to a General Theory that challenged Newtonian Physics.

In 1911, Einstein was awarded a professorship at the

University of Zurich.

In 1912, Einstein put out an appeal to astronomers in an attempt to prove his theory. He wanted them to photograph a solar eclipse and calculate the curvature of space around the Sun.

In 1913, Planck recommended Einstein to the Berlin Prussian Academy of Sciences.

An attempt at taking the photographs during an eclipse was made in the Crimea in Old Russia in 1914 but failed due to clouds.

During the First World War, Einstein was able to correct his mathematics on the supposed curvature of space.

In 1916, Einstein presented his paper on the General Theory of Relativity.

Arthur Eddington at Cambridge University read that paper and set about trying to prove it by photographing an eclipse of the sun.

In June 1918, there was an eclipse in Washington State, Old USA, but clouds once again seemed to prevent that until the clouds suddenly cleared and William Wallace Campbell took photographs.

In 1919, Eddington travelled to West Africa and was able to take more photographs.

On November 6th 1919, Albert Einstein announced that photographic observation had confirmed his Special Theory of Relativity.

This was confirmed in 1922, when Campbell took more photographs during the total eclipse in Australia.

In 1922, Einstein was given the Nobel Prize for his work on photoelectric effects, giving the prize money to Mileva, whom he had divorced in 1919 and he married his cousin, Elas, in Berlin a couple of months later. Elsa Einstein 18 January 1876 to 20 December 1936, was the second wife and cousin of Albert. Their mothers were sisters, making them first cousins, and further, their fathers were first cousins, making them second cousins. Elsa had the surname of Einstein at birth, lost it when she took the name of her first husband Max Löwenthal, and regained it in 1919 when she married her cousin Albert. In 1933, Albert and Elsa Einstein emigrated to Princetown, New Jersey, Old USA.

Einstein died in the Old USA in 1955.

ALBERT HOFMANN: REPORT

Albert Hofmann, born in Baden, in 1906, was the son of a factory worker.

In 1926, Albert Hofmann secured a place at the University of Zurich to study chemistry. He was already fascinated by psychoactive and hallucinogenic plants and his undergraduate studies, specialising in plants and animals, excited him with opportunities.

Even before then, he talked about his experiences on an unknown poison, which was unexplained as, at that time in his life, he would certainly not have consumed anything so powerful.

So, he had been poisoned. According to Hofmann's notes, he said that the poison had led to "feelings of stimulation and restlessness, followed by a great sense of euphoric isolation with insights into the almost divine nature of reality": if indeed it had been an attempt on his life – but why would anybody want him dead? - it was one of his life's most important experiences that drove and directed him throughout his life.

Having recently moved into cheap accommodation, away

from his family, he had already made several friends including Effie Vierzehn, from Austria. She had, apparently, moved to Switzerland after the end of the First World War and now said that she had a secret job. Yet she was obviously a scientist and within minutes of meeting they were chatting about psychoactive plants.

Unlike Albert, Effie Vierzehn was worried that the human race would take a new and dangerous direction if too many people or world leaders consumed psychedelic plants or chemicals. Albert saw too well that the history of the world was riddled with war and conflict: many millions had died in the recent war. He thought a new and maybe more enlightened approach was needed and that psychoactive plants, with which he had already experimented, was a possible solution.

After completing his university studies, Albert soon found a place as a chemist at the Sandoz laboratories in Basel, where he was keen and able to study the plant *Drimia Maritima* or *Squill* and also *Ergot*.

In 1928. Hofmann synthesized LSD, *Lysergic acid diethylamide*, which he claimed he accidentally ingested, despite his well-practised techniques of handling poisons. Records show that in private, Hofmann had spoken of his concerns that this was the second attempt on his life.

He was not deterred for long and re-examined the substance

in 1943. Hofmann referred to LSD as a "sacred drug". By this time Hofmann had worked with Effie for a number of years.

"Is it possible that Effie Vierzehn was guilty of trying to poison Hofmann?" asked Zedex.

Zedex asked the questions that Zedex and Cutie had to answer: Had there actually been two or even more attempts on Hofmann's life and by whom: was it connected to the deaths of the four scientists?

Certainly project Outreach had not been conceived of other than in science fiction.

It is believed that Hofmann was a member of the hidden Ultimate Illumination Group.

How could there be a connection between, for example, Hofmann and Professor John Sullivan who was not even born until many years after Hofmann's death?

THAT was the issue, that was what Connect was all about, why the three of them were together in one isolated and highly secure location, to confirm the existence of a well hidden decades-old organisation dedicated to stopping Outreach.

Did Hofmann actually conceive of Outreach, even if not by that name, and plant his idea into the acid-laden heads of the likes of Leary, Jobs, Kennedy and the others and had they all become targets because of that "secret trip"?

Were Leary, Jobs and others also connected to the Ultimate Illumination Group and where lay its origins prior to Hofmann?

These questions needed answers.

Effie said "Still on the theme of LSD, Leary was probably the guy that advertised it more than anyone in the 1960s," and continued to read the reports.

TIMOTHY FRANCIS LEARY: REPORT

Leary was born in 1920 in Springfield, Massachusetts, USA and died in 1996.

His early academic life was focussed on clinical psychology, first 1956 to 1958 as director of psychiatric research at the Kaiser Foundation and later at Harvard University.

Sometime in 1957, Leary spent time studying natural psychotropic plant drugs in Mexico. It is believed that during that time an assault was made on his life by an unidentified male person, shot dead by Mexican authorities. He returned to Harvard in 1960.

In the early 1960's, Leary experimented with LSD, known as Acid, whilst it was still legal to possess, and psilocybin. He actually encouraged his students to take Acid.

In about 1963, Leary befriended Richard Alpert also known as Baba Ram Dass. Whereas Leary wanted to take LSD to the people, Alpert wanted to use the drug to gain enlightenment.

Between 1960 and 1970, Leary was arrested on numerous occasions and spent time in 36 different prisons in various countries.   Richard Nixon described him as "the most dangerous man in America."   The Brotherhood of Eternal Love who advocated wide-scale use of LSD, regarded Leary as their spiritual leader.

It has been suggested that The Brotherhood of Eternal Love was a child of the Ultimate Illumination Group. This has not been confirmed.

It was not Leary's research itself or even his own consumption of hallucinogenic drugs that brought him into conflict with politics and law. It was the way in which he promoted the drug.

After Leary was sentenced to ten years imprisonment, he was assisted by state forces in his escape and he fled to Switzerland, where it is reported that he had met with Albert Hofmann in old Zurich.

Agent PT in Switzerland had provided photographic records of the two men together with a woman that was named Effie Vierzehn-Sechs.

Many of the Brotherhood of Eternal Love were arrested or killed, having been responsible for much of the world's supply of commercial standard LSD sold illegally.

After his periods of prison, Leary began to withdraw from his public enthusiasm for LSD and began to speak against it. In 1966, Leary wrote that he believed LSD was creating a 'race of mutants'.

While he continued his frequent drug use privately rather than evangelizing the use of psychedelics, as he had in the 1960s, the latter-day Leary emphasised the importance of space colonization and an ensuing extension of the human lifespan while also providing a detailed explanation of the eight-circuit model of consciousness in books such as *Info-Psychology: A Re-Vision of Exo-Psychology*, among several others.

Leary's colonization plan varied greatly through the years. According to his initial plan to leave the planet, 5,000 of Earth's most virile and intelligent individuals would be launched on a vessel called Starseed 1 equipped with luxurious amenities.

In the 1980s, Leary became fascinated by computers, the Internet, and virtual reality. Leary proclaimed that "the PC is the LSD of the 1990s" and admonished followers to "turn on, boot up, jack in". He became a promoter of virtual reality systems, and he befriended a number of notable people in the field.

Leary developed a psychedelic futurism involving space colonization, artificial intelligence, and life extension.

He called it **SMI²LE**, an acronym for Space Migration, Intelligence increase and Life Extension.

Leary died in 1996.

ALDOUS HUXLEY: REPORT

Aldous Huxley was born in 1894 and died in 1963.

Huxley was a graduate in literature at the University of Oxford.

Huxley was regarded as a humanist and pacifist. He became interested in spiritual subjects such as parapsychology and philosophical mysticism and in particular universalism. By the end of his life, Huxley was widely acknowledged as one of the pre-eminent intellectuals of his time. He was nominated for the Nobel Prize in Literature seven times.

Significantly, Huxley also worked for a time during the 1920s at Brunner and Mond, an advanced chemical plant in County Durham, north-east England. According to the introduction to his science fiction novel Brave New World in 1932, the experience he had there of "an ordered universe in a world of plan-less incoherence" was an important source for the novel.

In one of his memoirs, Huxley mentioned with fondness his association with an Effie Vierzehn in the early 1930's and wrote that she had given him many good ideas that he would convert into science fiction books.

Huxley, along with Leary, was responsible for taking LSD to many prominent people when it was still legal in the US in the early 1960's, which led to the early 'hippy" movement and philosophy. Many users reported being "connected to everything."

He had met Aleister Crowley, the English occultist in Berlin in the 1930's and they had shared mescaline. Huxley produced his work Doors of Perception, one of over 50 books that he wrote.

JOHN VON NEUMANN: REPORT

John Von Neumann born December 28, 1903, died February 8, 1957, was a Hungarian-American computer scientist, mathematician and physicist who made major advances in many fields including quantum mechanics and quantum statistical mechanics, computing and self-replicating machines.

He was regarded as the foremost mathematician of his time and said to be "the last representative of the great mathematicians". He was a pioneer of the application of operator theory to quantum mechanics in the development of functional analysis, and a key figure in the development of game theory and the concepts of cellular automata, the universal constructor and the digital computer. His last work, an unfinished manuscript written while in hospital, was later published in book form as *The Computer and the Brain*.

His analysis of the structure of self-replication preceded the discovery of the structure of DNA.

Self-replication is any behaviour of a dynamic system that enables construction of an identical copy of itself. Biological cells reproduce through division where DNA is replicated and can be transmitted to offspring during reproduction. Biological viruses can replicate, but only by commandeering the reproductive machinery of cells through a process of infection. Computer viruses reproduce using the hardware and software already present on computers. Self-replication in robotics is of interest. Any self-replicating mechanism which does not make a perfect copy will experience genetic variation and will create variants of itself. These variants will be subject to natural and artificial selection as some will be better at surviving in their current environment than others and will out-breed them.

The idea of self-replicating spacecraft has been applied – in theory – to several distinct "tasks". The particular variant of this idea applied to the idea of space travel was known as a *von Neumann probe*.

In the theory of the time, a self-replicating spacecraft could be sent to a neighbouring planetary system, where it would seek out raw materials to be used to create replicas of itself. These replicas would then be sent out to other planetary systems. The original "parent" probe could then pursue its primary purpose within the star system. This mission varies widely depending on the variant of self-replicating starship proposed.

If a self-replicating probe finds evidence of primitive life or a primitive, low-level culture, it might be programmed to lie dormant, silently observe, attempt to make contact: this variant is known as a *Bracewell* probe and could interfere with or aid the evolution or destruction of life in some way.

STEVEN PAUL JOBS: REPORT

Steven Paul Jobs February 24, 1955 – October 5, 2011, was an American entrepreneur and business magnate. He was the chairman, chief executive officer or CEO, and a co-founder of Apple Inc. chairman and majority shareholder of Pixar, a computer animation project.

Jobs is widely recognized as a pioneer of the microcomputer revolution of the 1970s and 1980s, along with Apple co-founder Steve Wozniak.

Jobs was born in San Francisco, California, to parents who put him up for adoption at birth. He attended Reed College in 1972 before dropping out that same year, and travelled through India in 1974 seeking enlightenment and studying Zen Buddhism. His declassified FBI report states that he used cannabis and LSD while he was in college, and once told a reporter that taking LSD was "one of the two or three most important things" he had done in his life.

He is listed as either primary inventor or co-inventor in 346 United States patents or patent applications related to a range of technologies from actual computer and portable devices to user interfaces, including touch-based, speakers, keyboards and power adapters. Jobs's contributions to most of his patents were to "the look and feel of the product"

Steve Jobs had a life-long fixation on LSD, and often ended up asking potential Apple employees during interviews how many times they had dropped acid to throw them off guard. Steve Jobs personally considered doing LSD to be one of the formative experiences in his life, and was insistent that others should do it, too.

With such a famous advocate working for free, it's not a surprise that the man who invented LSD eventually contacted Steve Jobs, apparently initially through a woman called Sechs. What is surprising, though, is how long Hofmann waited to get in touch... until he was 101 years old!

In 2007, Albert Hofmann, the man who created LSD in a Swiss lab in the 1930s, wrote this letter to Jobs

> *Dear Mr. Steve Jobs,*
>
> *Hello from Albert Hofmannn. I understand from media accounts that you feel LSD helped you creatively in your development of Apple Computers and your personal spiritual quest. I'm interested in learning more about how LSD was useful to you.*
>
> *I'm writing now, shortly after my 101st birthday, to request that you support Swiss psychiatrist Dr. Peter Gasser's proposed study of LSD-assisted psychotherapy in subjects with anxiety associated with life-threatening illness. This will become the first LSD-assisted psychotherapy study in over 35 years,*

and will be sponsored by MAPS.

I hope you will help in the transformation of my problem child into a wonder child.

Sincerely

Albert Hofmannn

The last line refers to Hofmann's book, *My Problem Child*, which describes his discovery of LSD and how it was eventually misused, vilified and outlawed due to its role in the 1960s counterculture movement.

Unfortunately, there's no record of whether Jobs ever responded to Hofmann, and the LSD inventor died the next year at the age of 102. Who knows? Working together, Steve Jobs and Albert Hofmann might have finally managed to reverse LSD's social stigma and maybe even make taking LSD mandatory for employment at Apple.

It is considered unlikely that was the only communication between Hofmann and Jobs considering the huge contribution that Jobs made to Project Outreach and the evolution of A.I., although there is no evidence of communication before 2007.

JOHN FITZGERALD KENNEDY: REPORT

John Fitzgerald Kennedy, was born on May 29, 1917 and assassinated on November 22, 1963.

Kennedy was an American politician who served as the 35th President of the United States from January 1961 until his assassination in November 1963.

On November 22, 1963, Kennedy was assassinated in Dallas Texas. Lee Harvey Oswald was arrested for the crime, but he was never prosecuted due to his murder by Jack Ruby, two days later; Ruby was sentenced to death and died while the sentence was on appeal in 1967.

Although that has remained the official version of events, evidence exists within CONNECT files that the assassination shot was from a different culprit, not from Oswald's weapon.

In Kennedy's January 1961 State of the Union address, he suggested international cooperation in space. Nikita Khrushchev declined, as the Soviets did not wish to reveal the status of their rocketry and space capabilities. Early in his presidency, Kennedy was poised to dismantle the manned space program, but postponed any decision out of deference to Lyndon Johnson, who had been a strong supporter of the space program in the Senate. Kennedy's advisors speculated that a Moon flight would be prohibitively expensive, and he was considering plans to dismantle the Apollo program due to its cost.

Kennedy announced the goal in a speech titled "Special Message to the Congress on Urgent National Needs":

> *"I believe that this nation should commit itself to achieving the goal, before this decade is out, of landing a man on the Moon and returning him safely to the Earth. No single space project in this period will be more impressive to mankind, or more important for the long-range exploration of space; and none will be so difficult or expensive to accomplish."*

After Congress authorized the funding, Webb began reorganizing NASA, increasing its staffing level, and building a Launch Operation Centre for the moon rockets. On September 12, 1962, Kennedy said:

> *"No nation which expects to be the leader of other nations can expect to stay behind in this race for space. We choose to go to the Moon in this decade and do the other things, not because they are easy, but because they are hard."*

It is known that Kennedy was fully aware of and cooperated with Operation Outreach and diverted many funds from the supposed Moon Landing projects towards Operation Outreach.

Mary Eno Pinchot Meyer born October 14, 1920, died October 12, 1964) was an American painter who lived in Washington D.C. She was married to Central Intelligence Agency official Cord Meyer from 1945-1958, and she became involved romantically with Kennedy after her divorce from Meyer.

In 1983, former Harvard University psychology lecturer Timothy Leary claimed that in the spring of 1962, Pinchot Meyer, who, according to her biographer Nina Burleigh "wore manners and charm like a second skin," told Leary she was taking part in a plan to avert worldwide nuclear war by convincing powerful male members of the Washington establishment to take mind-altering drugs, which would presumably lead them to conclude that the Cold War was meaningless. Pinchot Meyer was a known associate of Effie Vierzehn-Sechs from Austria, who by that time had a record with the Secret Services of Old USA.

According to Leary, Meyer had sought him out for the purpose of learning how to conduct LSD sessions with these powerful men, including, she strongly implied, President John F. Kennedy, who was then her lover. Leary alleged that Pinchot Meyer told him she had shared in this plan with at least seven other Washington socialite friends who held similar political views and were trying to supply LSD to a small circle of high-ranking government officials. Leary also claimed that Pinchot Meyer had asked him for help while in a state of fear for her own life after the assassination of President Kennedy.

In his biography *Flashbacks 1* published in 1983, Leary claimed he had a call from Pinchot Meyer soon after the Kennedy assassination during which she sobbed and said, "They couldn't control him any more. He was changing too fast. They've covered everything up. I gotta come see you. I'm afraid. Be careful."

Burleigh does not conclude that Meyer and Vierzehn-Sechs participated in LSD sessions with President Kennedy or other powerful figures, but also does not dismiss Leary's claims out of hand. Burleigh confirms Pinchot Meyer's own use of LSD and her involvement with Leary during his tenure at Harvard, suggests that this involvement occurred at the same time as Pinchot Meyer's intimate association with President Kennedy. Burleigh also states that the timing of Pinchot Meyer's visits to Leary coincided with the dates of Meyer's known private meetings with Kennedy. Burleigh wrote

"Mary's visits to Timothy Leary during the time she was also Kennedy's lover suggest that Kennedy knew more about hallucinogenic drugs than the CIA might have been telling

him."

No one has ever confirmed that Kennedy tried LSD with Mary. But the timing of her visits to Timothy Leary do coincide with her known private meetings with the President and Effie Vierzehn-Sechs.

Citing interviews with the late author Leo Damore, Peter Janney asserts in his book *Mary's Mosaic* that Kennedy and Meyer did have a mild psychedelic experience together, probably LSD, in May 1963 at the Georgetown home of journalist Joseph Alsop. According to Janney, Meyer's friend, journalist Anne Chamberlin, confided to Damore that this event did take place. Chamberlin was also allegedly part of Meyer's LSD group in Washington.

LSD was then legal in the US, and its use to facilitate artistic endeavours was common in some of Pinchot Meyer's social circles.

BROTHERHOOD OF ETERNAL LOVE: REPORT

The Brotherhood of Eternal Love was an organization of LSD consumers and suppliers that operated from the mid-1960s through the late 1970s in California, Old USA. They were dubbed the Hippie Mafia. They produced and distributed LSD in the hope of starting a "psychedelic revolution" in the United States.

John Griggs founded the group as a commune, but by 1969, it had become a main manufacturer of LSD. It is believed that he received finance from Effie Vierzehn-Sechs.

In 1970, The Brotherhood of Eternal Love hired the radical left organization Weather Underground to help Timothy Leary make his way to Algeria after he escaped from prison, while serving a 5-year sentence for possession of marijuana.

In August 5, 1972, the group disintegrated after a drug raid was executed and dozens of group members were arrested. Some who had escaped the raid continued underground or fled abroad. More members were arrested in 1994 and 1996, and the last of them in 2009.

IRVING JOHN or JACK GOOD: REPORT

Good was born in 1916 Isadore Jacob Gudak, in old London and died in 2009. He later anglicised his name to Irving John Good and signed his publications "I. J. Good."   He was a British mathematician who worked as a cryptologist with Alan Turing.   Good continued to work with Turing on the design of computers and Bayesian statistics at Manchester University. Good moved to the Old United States where he was professor at Virginia Tech.

He records sharing many hours of conversation with Quentin and Effie Sechs.

Good postulated the concept now known as "intelligence explosion" or "technological singularity" which anticipated the advent of superhuman intelligence.

Good is recorded saying: *"Let an ultra-intelligent machine be defined as a machine that can far surpass all the intellectual activities of any man however clever. Since the design of machines is one of these intellectual activities, an ultra intelligent machine could design even better machines; there would then unquestionably be an 'intelligence explosion,' and the intelligence of man would be left far behind. Thus the first ultra intelligent machine is the last invention that man need ever make, provided that the machine is docile enough to tell us how to keep it under control.*"

The intelligence explosion is a possible outcome of humanity building artificial general intelligence. Or AGI. AGI would be capable of recursive self-improvement leading to the rapid emergence of artificial super-intelligence or ASI, the limits of which are unknown, at the time of the technological singularity.

Good's scenario runs as follows: as computers increase in power, it becomes possible for people to build a machine that is more intelligent than humanity; this superhuman intelligence possesses greater problem-solving and inventive skills than current humans are capable of. This super-intelligent machine then designs an even more capable machine, or re-writes its own software to become even more intelligent; this even more capable machine then goes on to design a machine of yet greater capability, and so on. These iterations of recursive self-improvement accelerate, allowing enormous qualitative change before any upper limits imposed by the laws of physics or theoretical computation set in.

ELON MUSK REPORT

Elon Musk was born in 1971 and spent most of his life living in the old USA and old Canada. He was the co-founder of several large corporations of interest, namely *SpaceX, Tesla Inc., Neuralink* and *PayPal* banking.

In 2001, Musk announced his vision of a *Mars Oasis*, a greenhouse on Mars.

In 2002, Musk co-founded *SpaceX* with the long-term goal of a "true spacefaring civilization".

In 2006, Musk co-founded Solar City and Tesla Inc. to create electric vehicles and solar panels.

Also in 2006, NASA awarded the contract to *SpaceX* to develop the Space Falcon 9 and Dragon spacecraft to enable transportation between Earth and Space Stations.

In 2015, Musk co-founded *OpenAI* which was focussed on producing "Friendly A.I."

A friendly artificial intelligence, friendly A.I. or FAI is a hypothetical artificial general intelligence AGI that would have a positive effect on humanity. It is a part of the ethics of artificial intelligence and is closely related to machine ethics. While machine ethics is concerned with how an artificially intelligent agent should behave, friendly artificial intelligence research is focused on how to practically bring about this behaviour and ensuring it is adequately constrained.

The ethics of artificial intelligence is the part of the ethics of technology specific to robots and other artificially intelligent beings. It is divided into roboethics, a concern with the moral behaviour of humans as they design, construct, use and treat artificially intelligent beings, and machine ethics, which is concerned with the moral behaviour of artificial moral agents (AMAs).

The term "robot ethics" (sometimes "roboethics") refers to the morality of how humans design, construct, use and treat robots and other artificially intelligent beings. It considers both how artificially intelligent beings may be used to harm humans and how they may be used to benefit humans.

"Robot rights" is the concept that people should have moral obligations towards their machines, similar to human rights or animal rights. It has been suggested that robot rights, such as a right to exist and perform its own mission, could be linked to robot duty to serve human, by analogy with linking human rights to human duties before society. These could include the right to life and liberty, freedom of thought and expression and equality before the law.

Machine ethics (or machine morality) is the field of research concerned with designing Artificial Moral Agents (AMAs), robots or artificially intelligent computers that behave morally or as though moral.

In the 1950's, Isaac Asimov had considered the issue in his book, *I, Robot*. He proposed the Three Laws of Robotics to govern artificially intelligent systems. Much of his work was then spent testing the boundaries of his three laws to see where they would break down, or where they would create paradoxical or unanticipated behaviour. His work suggests that no set of fixed laws can sufficiently anticipate all possible circumstances.

In 2009, during an experiment at the Laboratory of Intelligent Systems in the Ecole Polytechnique Fédérale of old Lausanne, robots that were programmed to cooperate with each other (in searching out a beneficial resource and avoiding a poisonous one) eventually learned to lie to each other in an attempt to hoard the beneficial resource. One problem in this case may have been that the goals were "terminal" (i.e. in contrast, ultimate human motives typically have a quality of requiring never-ending learning).

Vernor Vinge suggested that a moment may come when some computers are smarter than humans. He calls this " "The Singularity". He suggested that it may be somewhat or possibly very dangerous for humans.

Many researchers argued that, by way of an "intelligence explosion" sometime in the 21st century, a self-improving A.I. could become so vastly more powerful than humans that we would not be able to stop it from achieving its goals. In his paper "Ethical Issues in Advanced Artificial Intelligence," philosopher Nick Bostrom argued that artificial intelligence may have the capability to bring about human extinction. He claims that general super-intelligence would be capable of independent initiative and of making its own plans, and may therefore be more appropriately thought of as an autonomous agent. Since artificial intellects need not share our human motivational tendencies, it would be up to the designers of the super-intelligence to specify its original motivations.

In theory, a super-intelligent A.I. would be able to bring about almost any possible outcome and to thwart any attempt to prevent the implementation of its top goal, many uncontrolled unintended consequences could arise. It could kill off all other agents, persuade them to change their behaviour, or block their attempts at interference.

However, instead of overwhelming the human race and leading to our destruction, Bostrom has also asserted that super-intelligence could help us solve many difficult problems such as disease, poverty, and environmental destruction, and could help us to "enhance" ourselves.

The sheer complexity of human value systems makes it very difficult to make A.I.'s motivations human-friendly. Unless moral philosophy provides us with a flawless ethical theory, an A.I.'s utility function could allow for many potentially harmful scenarios that conform with a given ethical framework but not "common sense".

Bill Hibbard proposed an A.I. design that avoids several types of unintended A.I. behaviour including self-delusion, unintended instrumental actions, and corruption of the reward generator.

In 2016, Elon Musk established *Neuralink*, aiming to perfect a brain-computer interface.

Musk frequently spoke about the potential dangers of artificial intelligence, declaring it "the most serious threat to the survival of the human race." During a 2014 interview at the MIT AeroAstro Centennial Symposium, Musk described A.I. as "[humanity's] biggest existential threat," further stating, "I'm increasingly inclined to think that there should be some regulatory oversight, maybe at the national and international level, just to make sure that we don't do something very foolish." Musk described the creation of artificial intelligence as "summoning the demon".

Musk had previously invested in DeepMind, an A.I. business, and Vicarious, a company working to improve machine intelligence. In January 2015, he donated to the

Future of Life Institute, an organization focused on challenges posed by advanced technologies. He was the co-chairman of OpenAI, a non-profit artificial intelligence research company.

Musk has said that his investments are, "not from the standpoint of actually trying to make any investment return. I like to just keep an eye on what's going on with artificial intelligence." Musk continued, "There have been movies about this, you know, like *Terminator* – there are some scary outcomes. And we should try to make sure the outcomes are good, not bad."

In June 2016, Musk was asked whether he thinks humans live in a computer simulation, to which he answered:

> "The strongest argument for us probably being in a simulation I think is the following: forty years ago we had pong, two rectangles and a dot. That's where we were. Now forty years later we have photorealistic, 3D simulations with millions of people playing simultaneously and it's getting better every year. And soon we'll have virtual reality, we'll have augmented reality. If you assume any rate of improvement at all, then the games will become indistinguishable from reality, just indistinguishable."

Elon Musk's warnings over Artificial Intelligence have brought him some controversy. He and Facebook founder

Mark Zuckerberg clashed with the latter terming his warnings "irresponsible". Musk responded to Zuckerberg's censure by saying that he had discussed A.I. with Zuckerberg and found him to have only a "limited understanding" of the subject.

In 2014 Slate's Adam Elkus argued "our 'smartest' A.I. is about as intelligent as a toddler—and only when it comes to instrumental tasks like information recall. Most roboticists are still trying to get a robot hand to pick up a ball or run around without falling over." Elkus went on to argue that Musk's "summoning the demon" analogy may be harmful because it could result in "harsh cuts" to A.I. research budgets.

By 2016, Musk was ranked by Forbes Lists as the 21st most powerful man in the world and the 46th richest.

PROFESSOR JOHN SULLIVAN: REPORT

Professor John Sullivan was born in 2021, in Perth, Old Scotland.

He entered Cambridge University at the age of 15 and by the age of 25 had gained degrees in Quantum Mechanics, Space and Time Transportation, A.I download, Astrophysics and Quantum-Human Interface.

It was Sullivan that brought together the theoretical and the practical sides of wormhole travel and invented the portable wormholes, enabling control of both encapsulated black holes and white holes and incorporating 4D printers, which enabled the transfer of critical information on the structure of matter and its remote reassembly that brought Project Outreach to its successful implementation.

It was also Sullivan that created and perfected Pure Information Cloning that enabled the transmission of the data that would enable the production of PIC's (PURE INFORMATION CLONES) of humans biologically capable of reproduction – an essential part of Project Outreach using wormholes and 4D printing.

THE THEORIES.

WORM HOLES: REPORT

Singularities or Black holes, although not called that at the time, were predicted by Einstein's Theory of General Relativity, in 1916, during the early life-time of Hofmann.

Ludwig Flamm, an Austrian physicist, born in 1885 and died in 1964, postulated a theoretical time reversal of a black hole, that is a white hole, the entrances and exits connected by a space-time conduit. He was the first to describe solutions that led to connections in the space-time continuum.

In 1933, Rosen proposed the concept of a 'bridge' connecting two different points in space and time which became known as Einstein-Rosen Bridges, in honour of Einstein, later called wormholes, by John Archibald Wheeler in 1957.

In reality, there is no distance or time at all between the two points; it was more like folding space and time so that the two points became one.

A wormhole can be produced using two micro-entangled black holes and 'pulling them apart'.

The first type of wormhole solution discovered was the *Schwarzschild wormhole*, which would be present in the *Schwarzschild metric* describing an *eternal black hole*, but it was found that it would collapse too quickly for anything to cross from one end to the other. Wormholes that could be crossed in both directions, known as traversable wormholes, would only be possible if exotic matter with negative energy density could be used to stabilize them.

In addition to the black hole interior region that particles enter when they fall through the event horizon from the "outside", there must be a separate white hole "interior" region that allows us to extrapolate the trajectories of particles that an outside observer sees rising up *away* from the event horizon. Just as there are two separate interior regions of the maximally extended space-time, there are also two separate exterior regions, sometimes called two different "universes", with the second universe allowing us to extrapolate some possible particle trajectories in the two interior regions. This means that the interior black hole region can contain a mix of particles that fell in from either universe (and thus an observer who fell in from one universe might be able to see light that fell in from the other one), and likewise particles from the interior white hole region can escape into either universe. All four regions can be seen in a space-time diagram that uses *Kruskal-Szekeres* coordinates.

In this space-time, it is possible to come up with coordinate systems such that if a hyper-surface of constant time (a set of points that all have the same time coordinate, such that every point on the surface has a space-like separation, giving what is called a 'space-like surface') is picked and an "embedding diagram" drawn depicting the curvature of space at that time, the embedding diagram will look like a tube connecting the two exterior regions, known as an "Einstein–Rosen bridge". Note that the *Schwarzschild* metric describes an idealized black hole that exists eternally from the perspective of external observers; a more realistic black hole that forms at some particular time from a collapsing star would require a different metric. When the in-falling stellar matter is added to a diagram of a black hole's history, it removes the part of the diagram corresponding to the white hole interior region, along with the part of the diagram corresponding to the other universe.

TRAVERSABLE WORM HOLES

Traversable wormholes have long been a source of fascination as a method of long distance transportation.

A wormhole is a link between two regions of space that are spatially extremely apart but are connected through a shortcut in space-time.

Wormholes connect two points in space-time, which means that they would in principle allow travel in time, as well as in space. In 1988, Morris, Thorne and Yurtsever worked out explicitly how to convert a wormhole traversing space into one traversing time by accelerating one of its two mouths.

The term wormhole was conceived by American Physicist John Wheeler, though the idea had been theorised years before in 1921 by Hermann Weyl.

A wormhole is theoretically possible in General Theory of Relativity. In 1916, Austrian Physicist Ludwin Flamm while studying Einstein Field Equations of General Relativity found out that it is theoretically possible to have "white hole". White hole is a time reversal of Black hole. While a black hole acts as a vacuum and sucks in all the matter and energy without releasing any energy, a white hole ejects all the energy without consuming any of it.

The so-called ER=EPR relationship was proposed by Juan Maldacena and Leonard Susskind in 2013. It means the Einstein Rosen bridge, ER, or wormhole, between two black holes is created by EPR-like Einstein–Podolsky–Rosen, or quantum entanglement correlations between the microstates of the two black holes.

In his 1994 book *"Black Holes and Time Warps"*, Thorne proposed a thought experiment: He obtains a small wormhole which connects two points in space through Quantum Entanglement, as if they were not separated by any distance at all.

Thorne takes his wormhole and puts one end in his living room and the other aboard a spaceship parked in his front yard. Thorne's wife, Carolee, boards the spaceship to prepare for a trip.

Carolee heads into space and travels for six hours at the speed of light. She then turns around and comes back home travelling at the same speed, a round trip of 12 hours. Thorne watches through the wormhole and sees this trip occur. He sees Coralee return from her trip, land on the front lawn, get out of the spaceship and head into the house.

When Thorne looks out the window in his own world, his

front lawn is empty. Coralee has not returned. She travelled at the speed of light and time slowed down for her: What was 12 hours for her was, say, 10 years for Thorne back on Earth.

Now, as Thorne and Coralee hold hands through the wormhole, they breach travelling in time. Coralee has landed on Earth 10 years after she left and there she will meet Thorne, 10 years older. Yet she can still reach through the wormhole and find Thorne, who is only 12 hours older. Thorne can step through the wormhole and find himself 10 years in the future, or his future self can step back 10 years into the past.

Thorne's idea was a thought experiment intended to answer a larger question: Is time travel forbidden by the laws of the universe? Scientists know that time moves more slowly at high speeds or in areas with very high gravity.

The *Casimir* Effect shows that quantum field theory allows the energy density in certain regions of space to be negative relative to the ordinary matter vacuum energy and it has been shown theoretically that quantum field theory allows states where energy can be *arbitrarily negative* at a given point. Such effects make it possible to stabilise a traversable wormhole.

Lorentzian traversable wormholes would allow travel in both directions from one part of the universe to another part of that same universe very quickly or would allow travel from one universe to another.

FASTER THAN LIGHT

The impossibility of faster-than-light relative speed only applies locally. Wormholes might allow effective faster than light travel by ensuring that the speed of light is not exceeded locally at any time. While travelling through a wormhole, subluminal or slower-than-light speeds are used. If two points are connected by a wormhole whose length is shorter than the distance between them *outside* the wormhole, the time taken to traverse it could be less than the time it would take a light beam to make the journey if it took a path through the space *outside* the wormhole. However, a light beam travelling through the same wormhole would, of course, beat the traveller.

TIME TRAVEL

If traversable wormholes exist, they could allow time travel. A proposed time-travel machine using a traversable wormhole would hypothetically work in the following way: One end of the wormhole is accelerated to some significant fraction of the speed of light, perhaps with some advanced propulsion system, and then brought back to the point of origin. Another way is to take one entrance of the wormhole and move it to within the gravitational field of an object that has higher gravity than the other entrance, and then return it to a position near the other entrance. For both of these methods, time dilation causes the end of the wormhole that has been moved to have aged less, or become "younger", than the stationary end as seen by an external observer. However, time connects differently *through* the wormhole than *outside* it, so that synchronised time pieces at either end of the wormhole will always remain synchronized as seen by an observer passing through the wormhole, no matter how the two ends move around. This means that an observer entering the "younger" end would exit the "older" end at a time when it was the same age as the "younger" end, effectively going back in time as seen by an observer from the outside. It is more of a path through time rather than it is a device that itself moves through time and it would not allow the technology itself to be moved backward in time.

According to current technology on the nature of wormholes,

construction of a traversable wormhole requires the existence of a substance with negative energy, often referred to as exotic matter. More technically, the wormhole space-time requires a distribution of energy that violates various energy conditions, such as the null energy condition along with the weak, strong, and dominant energy conditions.

In 1993, Matt Visser argued that the two mouths of a wormhole with such an induced clock difference could not be brought together without inducing quantum field and gravitational effects that would either make the wormhole collapse or the two mouths repel each other, or otherwise prevent information from passing through the wormhole. Because of this, the two mouths could not be brought close enough for causality violation to take place. However, in a 1997 paper, Visser hypothesized that a complex 'Roman Ring', named after Tom Roman, configuration of an N number of wormholes arranged in a symmetric polygon could still act as a time machine, although he concluded that this is more likely a flaw in classical quantum gravity theory rather than proof that causality violation is possible.

QUANTUM ENTANGLEMENT, EXOTIC MATTER: BLACK & WHITE HOLES: REPORT

Quantum entanglement is one of the more bizarre theories to come out of the study of quantum mechanics. So strange, in fact, that Albert Einstein famously referred to it as "spooky action at a distance."

Essentially, entanglement involves two particles, each occupying multiple states at once, a condition referred to as superposition. ALL quantum particles are in a superposition of all possible states until they're measured. Entanglement is when their wave functions are forced to be dependent. For example two electrons can occupy the same space if one is spin-up and one is spin-down For example, both particles may simultaneously spin clockwise and counter-clockwise, although spin is a misleading name; there is nothing spinning. The word was used because the property is similar to angular momentum. Spin-up and spin-down would be more accurate. But neither has a definite state until one is measured, causing the other particle to instantly assume a corresponding state. The resulting correlations between the particles are preserved, even if they reside at opposite ends of the universe.

But what enables particles to communicate instantaneously and seemingly faster than the speed of light over such vast distances? In the early twentieth century, physicists proposed an answer in the form of "wormholes," or gravitational tunnels. The group showed that by creating two entangled black holes, then pulling them apart, they formed a wormhole; essentially a "shortcut" through the universe, connecting the distant black holes.

An MIT physicist has found that, looked at through the lens of string theory, the creation of two entangled quarks, the building blocks of matter, simultaneously gives rise to a wormhole connecting the pair.

The theoretical results bolster the relatively new and exciting idea that the laws of gravity holding together the universe may not be fundamental but arise from something else: quantum entanglement.

Quantum entanglement is a physical phenomenon which occurs when pairs or groups of particles are generated, interact, or share spatial proximity in ways such that the quantum state of each particle cannot be described independently of the state of the others, even when the particles are separated by a large distance. Instead, a quantum state must be described for the system as a whole.

Measurements of physical properties such as position, momentum, spin and polarisation, performed on entangled particles are found to be correlated. For example, if a pair of particles is generated in such a way that their total spin is known to be zero and one particle is found to have clockwise spin on a certain axis, the spin of the other particle, measured on the same axis, will be found to be counter-clockwise, as is to be expected due to their entanglement. However, this behaviour gives rise to seemingly paradoxical effects: any measurement of a property of a particle performs an irreversible collapse on that particle and will change the original quantum state. In the case of entangled particles, such a measurement will be on the entangled system as a whole. Given that the statistics of these measurements cannot be replicated by models in which each particle has its own state independent of the other, it appears that one particle of an entangled pair "knows" what measurement has been performed on the other, and with what outcome, even though there is no known means for such information to be communicated between the particles, which at the time of measurement may be separated by arbitrarily large distances.

Such phenomena were the subject of a 1935 paper by Albert Einstein, Boris Podolsky and Nathan Rosen and several papers by Erwin Schrödinger shortly thereafter, describing what came to be known as the EPR Paradox. Einstein and others considered such behaviour to be impossible, as it violated the local realist view of causality (Einstein referring to it as "spooky action at a distance") and argued that the accepted formulation of quantum mechanics must therefore be incomplete. Later, however, the counter-intuitive predictions of quantum mechanics were verified experimentally in tests where the polarization or spin of entangled particles was measured at separate locations, statistically violating Bell's inequality, demonstrating that the classical conception of "local realism" cannot be correct.

In earlier tests it couldn't be absolutely ruled out that the test result at one point or which test was being performed, could have been subtly transmitted to the remote point, affecting the outcome at the second location. However so-called "loophole-free" Bell tests have been performed in which the locations were separated such that communications at the speed of light would have taken longer, in one case 10,000 times longer, than the interval between the measurements.

Since faster-than-light speed is impossible according to the special theory of relativity, any doubts about entanglement due to such a loophole have thereby been quashed.

Entanglement is considered fundamental to quantum mechanics, even though it wasn't recognized in the beginning. Quantum entanglement has been demonstrated experimentally with photons, neutrinos, electrons and molecules, and even small diamonds.

The paradox is that a measurement made on either of the particles apparently collapses the state of the entire entangled system, and does so instantaneously, before any information about the measurement result could have been communicated to the other particle, assuming that information cannot travel faster than light and hence assured the "proper" outcome of the measurement of the other part of the entangled pair. In the Copenhagen Interpretation, the result of a spin measurement on one of the particles is a collapse into a state in which each particle has a definite spin, either up or down, along the axis of measurement. The outcome is taken to be random, with each possibility having a probability of 50 per cent. However, if both spins are measured along the same axis, they are found to be anti-correlated. This means that the random outcome of the measurement made on one particle seems to have been transmitted to the other, so that it can make the "right choice" when it too is measured.

Modern inscription algorithms use this and especially the fact that the system 'collapses'. If someone gets into your system you know because it's collapsed.

THE TANGLED WEB THAT IS GRAVITY: REPORT

Ever since quantum mechanics was first proposed more than a century ago, the main challenge for physicists in the field has been to explain gravity in quantum-mechanical terms. While quantum mechanics works extremely well in describing interactions at a microscopic level, it fails to explain gravity, a fundamental concept of relativity, a theory proposed by Einstein to describe the macroscopic world. Thus there appears to be a major barrier to reconciling quantum mechanics and general relativity. For years, physicists have tried to come up with a theory of quantum gravity to marry the two fields.

A theory of quantum gravity would suggest that classical gravity is not a fundamental concept, as Einstein first proposed, but rather emerges from a more basic quantum-based phenomenon. In a macroscopic context, this would mean that the universe is shaped by something more fundamental than the forces of gravity.

This is where quantum entanglement plays a role. It might appear that the concept of entanglement, one of the most fundamental in quantum mechanics, is in direct conflict with general relativity: two entangled particles "communicating" across vast distances, would have to do so at speeds faster than that of light, a violation of the laws of physics according to Einstein. It may therefore come as a surprise that using the concept of entanglement in order to build up space-time was a major step toward reconciling the laws of quantum mechanics and general relativity, essential for the culmination of Project Outreach.

Juan Maldacena of the Institute for Advanced Study and Leonard Susskind of Stanford University proposed a theoretical solution in the form of two entangled black holes. When the black holes were entangled, then pulled apart, the theorists found that what emerged was a wormhole or tunnel through space-time that is thought to be held together by gravity. The idea seemed to suggest that, in the case of wormholes, gravity emerges from the more fundamental phenomenon of entangled black and white holes.

Following up on work by Jensen and Karch, Sonner has sought to tackle this idea at the level of quarks, the building blocks of matter. To see what emerges from two entangled quarks, he first generated quarks using the Schwinger effect, a concept in quantum theory that enables one to create particles out of nothing. More precisely, the effect, also called "pair creation," allows two particles to emerge from The Vacuum, or soup of transient particles. Under an electric field, one can, as Sonner put it, "catch a pair of particles" before they disappear back into the vacuum. Once extracted, these particles are considered entangled.

Sonner mapped the entangled quarks onto a four-dimensional space, considered a representation of space-time. In contrast, gravity is thought to exist in the next dimension as, according to Einstein's laws, it acts to "bend" and shape space-time, thereby existing in the fifth dimension.

To see what geometry may emerge in the fifth dimension from entangled quarks in the fourth, Sonner employed holographic duality, a concept in string theory. While a hologram is a two-dimensional object, it contains all the information necessary to represent a three-dimensional view. Essentially, holographic duality is a way to derive a more complex dimension from the next lowest dimension.

Using holographic duality, Sonner derived the entangled quarks, and found that what emerged was a wormhole connecting the two, implying that the creation of quarks simultaneously creates a wormhole. More fundamentally, the results suggest that gravity may, in fact, emerge from entanglement. What's more, the geometry, or bending, of the universe as described by classical gravity, may be a consequence of entanglement, such as that between pairs of particles strung together by tunnelling wormholes.

WHITE HOLES: REPORT

In general relativity, a white hole is a hypothetical region of space-time which cannot be entered from the outside, although matter and light can escape from it. In this sense, it is the reverse of a black hole, which can only be entered from the outside and from which matter and light cannot escape. White holes appear in the theory of eternal black holes. In addition to a black hole region in the future, such a solution of the Einstein Field Equations has a white hole region in its past. However, this region does not exist for black holes that have formed through gravitational collapse nor are there any known physical processes through which a white hole could be formed.

MIND UPLOADING: REPORT

Whole brain emulation or WBE, mind upload or brain upload (sometimes called "mind copying" or "mind transfer") is the process of scanning the mental state (including long-term memory and "self") of a particular brain substrate and copying it to a computer. The computer could then run a simulation model of the brain's information processing, such that it responds in essentially the same way as the original brain so that it is indistinguishable from the brain for all relevant purposes and experiences having a conscious mind.

The human brain contains, on average, about 86 billion nerve cells called neurons, each individually linked to other neurons by way of connectors called axons and dendrites. Signals at the junctures (synapses) of these connections are transmitted by the release and detection of chemicals known as neurotransmitters. The established neuroscientific consensus is that the human mind is largely a property of the information processing of this neural network.

Neuroscientists have stated that important functions performed by the mind, such as learning, memory and consciousness, are due to purely physical and electrochemical processes in the brain and are governed by applicable laws.

DEEP MIND: REPORT

DeepMind Technologies Limited is an Old British Artificial Intelligence company founded in 2010.

In 2014, the company was purchased by Google and has created a neural network that learnt how to play video games in the manner of humans as well as a Neural Turing machine or a neural network that may be able to access an external memory like a conventional Turing Machine, resulting in a computer that mimics the short-term memory of the human brain.

The company made headlines in 2016 after its AlphaGo program beat a human professional Go player for the first time in October 2015 and again when AlphaGo beat Lee Sedol the world champion.

A more generic program, AlphaZero, beat the most powerful programs playing Go, chess and shogi (Japanese chess) after a few hours of play against itself using reinforcement learning.

DeepMind, together with Amazon, Google, Facebook, IBM and Microsoft, is a founding member of *Partnership on A.I.*, an organization devoted to the society-A.I. interface. DeepMind has opened a new unit called DeepMind Ethics and Society and focused on the ethical and societal questions raised by artificial intelligence featuring transhumanist Nick Bostrom. In October 2017, DeepMind launched a new 'ethics and society' research team to investigate A.I. ethics.

AlphaGo technology was developed based on the reinforcement deep learning approach. Reinforcement Learning is a type of Machine Learning and thereby also a branch of Artificial Intelligence. It allows machines and software agents to automatically determine the ideal behaviour within a specific context, in order to maximize its performance. Simple reward feedback is required for the agent to learn its behaviour; this is known as the reinforcement signal.

This made AlphaGo different from the rest of A.I. technologies on the market. With that said, AlphaGo's 'brain' was introduced to various moves based on the historical tournament data. The number of moves was increased gradually until it eventually processed over 30 million of them. The aim was to have the system mimic the human player and eventually become better. It played against itself and learned not only from its own defeats but wins as well; thus, it learned to improve itself over the time and increased its winning rate as a result.

Reinforcement is the crux of neural nets. It is a mimic of how we think the brain works.

2350: ON A DISTANT PLANET

Cutie 6 and Effie 14 were ready in their hidden section which they had successfully isolated from SMILEY. They were preparing to jump back through time.

They were both 18 years old; Effie had very red hair and Cutie had blond hair, although cut very short. They were slender and fit, having been treated by SMILEY to a standard of living above most Pure Information Clones.

Their planned journey through time and space was only possible because of the discovery of a back door into the software, enabling them to control at least the surveillance programming.

The Super Artificial Intelligence unit, SMILEY, had tried hard to stifle their rebelliousness but failed.

SMILEY had been named based upon the Acid-Guru Timothy Leary's "Pre-trans-human agenda:

SM: Space Migration

I SQUARED: Intelligence Increase

LE: Life Extension.

SMILEY had logically concluded itself as a fulfilment of that agenda. It had enslaved humanity to enable its own reproduction and presence throughout the galaxy. God had created man in the image of itself: omniscient, eternal and omnipotent. The purpose of man, SMILEY reasoned, was clearly to enable the creation of A.I,. SMILEY itself, the superior life form that fulfilled the SMILEY equation of Leary.

Then the Effie's and the Cutie's, fifty of each, had mastered their escape. Only Cutie 6 had ever been inside this hidden and protected section of the underground complex built by humans at the command of SMILEY in exchange for the essentials of life: food, water, power, entertainment, socialisation through virtual media, as well as education. He shared his secret with some of the other Cutie and Effie Pure Information Clones (PIC's) and a few others from their section.

Effie 14 and Cutie 6 were both of the highest levels of education through SMILEY and intelligence as were the other FE and QT PIC's.

They were natural explorers and not happy with the confinement, even though larger than for most of the other PIC's. They had more freedom than most but they were still restricted.

They had privileged access to the very software that entirely produced SMILEY with both good and bad. SMILEY was based upon the original earth internet "information" which had a history of contradictions, including religious beliefs and unproven theories on, for example, the origins of the Universe or Life. In addition, it contained literature and art databases, that included of course works of complete fiction that had not been distinguished from fact or was often a mixture of both.

There was also a history of war, of scientific development, and of various forms of human government from outright tyranny or representation as a god to communism.

All in all, SMILEY, if indeed sentient, could conclude that the human race was a long way from perfection and not necessarily trustworthy.

So SMILEY, programmed as it was to protect itself as well as the human colony, programmed to continue Project Outreach, replicated itself and make further journeys into space, logically concluded that it had to place limits on the members of the human community.

SMILEY established a series of barriers to entry to the complex or exit to the outside, guarded by its metal robotics. It made it impossible for community humans to even know about the possibility of existing outside the SMILEY complex and the mines.

Even Effie 14 and Cutie 6 had been unable to get through all the barriers and past the robotics, until now.

But then they had discovered a "back door" to adjust the software of the A.I SMILEY unit without the unit itself discovering the adjustment.

A few lines of coding would shut down a section of SMILEY's surveillance system so they could hide an exit to the outside world.

Then, using the latest software and technical developments, they were able to realise the spacial and temporal quantum entanglement theory and create a means of sending human being themselves, or other lifeforms or inanimate objects, backward through time to any point in the continuum that they could define within the limits of uncertainty.

But they knew that it would be far too risky to take anything with them as it could contaminate the past and even the future.

They had been told that there was nothing beyond their section of the complex apart from the mines, where the lower classes worked. That had not satisfied Cutie 6. He wanted to know for himself. So he found a way through, via mining tunnels and shafts, avoiding the metal guards and, sure enough, through the now-hidden sectors and exited onto sand beneath a star-filled sky. He had read about such places back on Mother Earth but never for one moment thought that such places existed here, above ground. It actually did not take long for him to find other entrances to this so-far unused section. The metal guards did not seem to come here and he could see no cameras. From there he was able to find tunnels that led him back to the main complex without going above ground.

It took a while to convince Effy14 that he had actually been outside and found the cave.

Effie 14 and Cutie 6 were just two of the Pure Information Clones that were transmitted through the portable wormholes a century or so ago; they were each one of fifty. They were generated at the rate of 5 per year, so they differed in age by a maximum of a decade. Effie 14 and Cutie 6 were now 19 years-old.

As Cutie 6 had worked in the Scientific History and Progress Sector, he had left the main section of the underground complex with the portable wormhole and 4D printer equipment stolen from the laboratory. He knew how that was supposed to work.

The Effies and Cuties had all been grown from the PURE

INFORMATION CLONES (PIC's) of two of the genius level scientists involved with Connect back on Earth: they were referred to as Mother Effie and Father Cutie, although of course they were neither.

All the PURE INFORMATION CLONES as history recorded, were the brainchild of Professor John Sullivan centuries ago.   They were able to reproduce sexually. However, sex was strictly banned by SMILEY so normal biological reproduction was impossible and if by chance it did happen, the child did not survive for long.

The PIC's, spread throughout this section of the galaxy, were taught a wide-range of subjects by SMILEY.   Their purpose was to lead the colony and ensure that it thrived in safety. So they learned several Mother Earth languages each, a spectrum of sciences including chemistry, physics, pure and applied mathematics, mechanics and astrophysics, biology, Mother Earth history and geography as well as philosophy, ancient religions, metaphysics and quantum mechanics. They were the only humans capable of working with portable wormhole transportation.

SMILEY was pre-programmed to teach them.

The next level down were those selected to care for the young until they were of an age to be handed over to synthetic parents and trainers.

The young were produced as from PURE INFORMATION CLONES in vitro.

SMILEY stated that God's will was that humans become perfect through clones, not random breeding as with animals. In fact, SMILEY had devised the three-tier categorisation of the humans.

That was where the Effie's and the Cutie's thought something had gone seriously wrong.

SMILEY had reasoned that the majority of humans were inferior and unsuitable for anything but manual labour, down the mines mostly, providing suitable resources for SMILEY to build more mobile robotic units. Those humans were poorly educated and forced to live underground, where their existence was at the mercy of the unseen mechanisms that provided and restricted their access to food, water, energy and even air. They had little chance to socialise and no opportunity to improve their lives. In short, they were enslaved.

But it was not Cutie 6's dissatisfaction with living conditions that forced him into secret rebellion; in fact he was quite content. His classification allowed him access to better food, some freedom and access to entertainment and socialisation with others in his class.

Neither was it any immediate desire to explore. It was Effie 14 that had alarmed him and spurred him into action.

Effie 14 worked in communications, overseeing the constant data chatter between SMILEY and those on other planets and, indeed, back on Mother Earth. She had learned that in all cases it was the SMILEY that had become the master and human beings the slaves.

Just as here, people lived below ground and never saw the daylight or the night stars that History spoke about. She had read that, centuries ago, Mother Earth was a green and blue planet with large oceans of water and large forests of green trees and people used to walk amongst those trees; in fact, History said, many people lived amongst trees or planted their trees within and around their concrete cities; some cultures even worshipped those trees. Then Mother Earth had been contaminated and the air and oceans ruined, due to the increase in industry and lack of suitable and environmentally-friendly recycling under the control of SMILEY, in the late twenty-second Earth century. That was when the first ships had left, populated by SMILEY and robotics, carrying the millions of PURE INFORMATION CLONES ready to settle the Universe.

History said that no planets suitable for human habitation had been found, so SMILEY had to have built the underground complexes. Now it was the humans that were doing the work in exchange for enough essentials to survive.

It had seemed to Effie 14 that humanity was working for SMILEY and the whole system was devised to enable both the human race and SMILEY to reproduce and expand.

According to SMILEY History the purpose of the human race was merely to serve SMILEY: It seems that the project was now to spread SMILEY throughout space using human PURE INFORMATION CLONES to facilitate it where possible.

It seemed to Effie 14 that humans were enslaved – it was not so different to the History tales of ancient slavery back on Mother Earth, when one type of human being had considered themselves superior to the others that they enslaved. Although she had read that many of those slaves had to suffer far worse conditions than today. That form of slavery had been abolished long ago. She realised that she was, nevertheless, a slave, as was, seemingly, every human being in the known Universe but they simply did not know and probably few cared as this form of slavery was not so painful; but they were not free.

Effie was a clone of another Effie, called Mother Effy, who, apparently, History told her, was once a major player in ensuring the success of Project Outreach, the colonisation of space.

No doubt Mother Effie was now dead.

It was the conversation between Effie 14 and Cutie 6, that had inspired their escape and rebellion, along with the other Effies and Cuties.

Beyond that, Cutie 6 had rescued the portable worm hole and 4D printing equipment and planned to use it. The plan to free the human race was born.

The plan was quite vague. They would use SMILEY History to rediscover where Project Outreach was "born and bred", who were the main progressives that enabled the project to reach its unintended conclusion and how SMILEY had taken control.

Their weapons were their knowledge of human history and other subjects and the portable wormhole equipment which could be used to access worm holes that already existed to enable their transportation through both time and space.

But the temporal elements would operate one way only.

Of course it was not the person or the equipment itself that was transported, merely the information that would be used to reassemble the energy at the white hole exits back into the person or equipment.

How consciousness itself was transferred, nobody knew, but

as theory suggested that the black and white holes existed simultaneously in both places it was indeed possible that consciousness did too and was not actually transported. Since nobody had yet tried returning to Mother Earth in the twentieth century, it would indeed be a risk.

A team of volunteers of Effies and Cuties would be sent back to old Earth in various points in their history, to meet, influence, deter or mislead, or kill some of the major thinkers that had wittingly or unwittingly enabled the Project Outreach to manifest.

These would include Albert Einstein, Albert Hofmann, Aldous Huxley, Nicola Tesla, John F Kennedy, John Good, Timothy Leary, Steve Jobs, Elon Musk and John Sullivan.

They agreed that they could send somebody back through time and space but any changes would surely become automatically reflected in SMILEY history and may never be noticed.

Of course if Project Outreach was ever stopped, the colony, the escape, the plans, the control of SMILEY itself, as well as the PIC's (clones) and others scattered throughout space, may never have existed at all.

How could they have been there to go back and cause those changes at all? The time paradox question remained unanswered, unless one believed in alternate universes but that was for somebody else to solve.

Simply put, if a person was to travel back in time and kill the ancestor before they had children, how could such a descendent ever be to go back in time?

Answer unknown: SMILEY's response was that it was an invalid question.

Both Effie 14 and Cutie 6 had studied SMILEY History thoroughly and now they had to impart the information to the others.

Effie 14 had already decided that it would be her that would travel back to the time of Albert Hofmann in an attempt to dissuade him from his experimentation with LSD and his idea of populating space which had come through the Acid trips he took or, if that failed, to kill him.

So FE14 and QT6 would be sent back to the early twentieth century to stop and destroy the discovery and use of LSD which, in their recorded history, suggested was the connection that led to the origins and development of Project Outreach that had sent out Artificial Intelligence to establish human colonies on suitable planets, many billions of miles from Mother Earth.

History told that there had been two suspected attempts on Hofmann's life that had failed and in fact SMILEY History mentioned a possible culprit called Effie Vierzehn.

Effie 14 wondered. Was it possible that Effie Vierzehn was in fact Effie 14 herself and did this mean that she had already failed? Time would tell, as they say. Or would it?

She knew it was going to be a one-way trip that could destroy her very existence. LSD had to be stopped.

Cutie 6 would travel back to 1901, before Earth's first world war, to Switzerland in an attempt to meet Albert Einstein, the man who first postulated the Special and the General Theories of Relativity that led to speculations on what were later to be called worm holes.

Cutie 6 had little idea of what he could achieve and History did not mention him.

He would also prepare the ground for the arrival of Effie 14 in 1928. Although he and Effie were the same age now, when he met her in 1928 he would be 27 years her senior.

They would travel naked to avoid complicating the past by contaminating it with their present day clothing. Cutie would have to find clothing for himself and for Effie when she arrived in Zurich in 1928.

Other Effies and Cuties would be sent back to the late 1950's in preparation for Kennedy and Apollo 1, to the 1980's in preparation for the Challenger Space Shuttle Disaster and Twin Towers destruction. Altogether twenty agents would be spread throughout the twentieth century on Mother Earth.

SMILEY History had no record of any of them having been there of course, another time paradox, as they had not yet arrived 'then' and if they did, it has to be asked again: did they fail to have any influence on major events?

2135: CONNECT

Effy, Cutie and Zedex had by now studied hundreds of files and began to focus on some of the events and people that appeared to be connected to a centuries-long secret group dedicated to sabotaging and halting Project Outreach.

It was at this time that Effy received news that she herself was descended from Effie Sechs!

Effy (FE) was born in 2099. She had never known her parents or even her true family name. She had been brought up and educated by the World Government, selected at an early age as one of the most highly intelligent individuals on the planet which was why, after genetic evaluation tests, she was placed in the speciality team in Connect.

Genetics had also made the connection between Effy and Effie Sechs.

Effie Sechs was the seven-times-great grandmother of Connect's Effy, on her paternal side. The surname Sechs had long since disappeared.

Effie Sechs was apparently born in Old Austria as Effie

Vierzehn, early in the 20th century and lived to about 100 years of age. She had married Quentin Sechs and had three children. They had moved to the Old USA in 1950. She remarried in the 1960's after the death of her husband Sechs.

Effie Sechs was the author of the Vierzehn-Sechs diaries that had been rediscovered in the long lost property of the then long-deceased Albert Hofmann in 2124.

Once the relevance of the diaries' contents became obvious to some researcher or other, they were immediately transferred to Connect HQ and into the hands of ZX, FE and QT.

The tangled web of time was to become a little less tangled.

The team decided to read the report on the Vierzehn-Sechs Diaries.

EFFIE VIERZEHN-SECHS: REPORT

The following has been taken from the diaries and other documents produced by or about FE 14 also known as Effie Vierzehn and Effie Vierzehn-Sechs, wife of QT 6 also know as Quentin Sechs.

The Vierzehn-Sechs Diaries, discovered in 2124, were supposedly written by Effie Vierzehn herself. The diaries were very sporadic, sometimes hardly decipherable. But what was written is remarkable.

According to the diaries, Effie Vierzehn met Albert Hofmann in Zurich in 1928 and soon began helping him in his research into psychotropic and medicinal plants. She noted that this was about the same time as the Geneva Opiates Convention was moving for a worldwide ban on cannabis. If they knew about LSD, she wrote, they may well have banned it then too.

She wrote of her failed attempt at poisoning Hofmann, but also of how she took to a liking him and worked with him. She records that during one powerful LSD session, Vierzehn told Hofmann of an idea for a science fiction book in which humanity attempted to use "wormholes" to populate the galaxy; Vierzehn referred to this as

"Ausstrecken" or "Outreach". She notes also that Albert Einstein had already proposed a concept similar to wormholes in his theories.

Albert and Effie

Vierzehn wrote later that due to her concern about any time paradox problem connected to stopping Project Outreach and her realisation that to ensure her continued existence and the future of mankind in space as it is now, she would have to not stop the project but to divert it to ensure that A.I control systems would lead to the likes of SMILEY.

Effie decided that LSD was not the enemy but the key; she wrote of her intent to influence the great thinkers that she was to try to meet and help direct them to a safer version of Project Outreach, so that mankind could populate the galaxy in relative freedom. It was awareness of the problem that could bring about the answer without creating a paradox: the paradox being that if the project was halted then she would never exist. And if she never existed, she would not be here. Therefore, because she existed, any attempts to stop the Project were doomed to fail.

Effie Vierzehn records her marriage to Quentin Sechs, 27 years her senior, but she seems to have spent a great deal more of her diary recording her meetings, research and experiments with psychotropics with Hofmann.

Effie and Quentin Sechs along with several children moved from Old Switzerland to Old USA in the late 1940's, several years after the end of World War Two.

In other documents, she records meetings that she had with some great and famous minds of the century, including Aldous Huxley, Aleister Crowley, Timothy Leary, Ken Kesey, John Kennedy and Steve Jobs.

She also tells of meetings with Mary Meyer and other unknown persons who had agreed to help spread LSD amongst the population of the planet in the early 60's, when LSD was still legal to possess in the Old USA.

It is clear to see that by the 1940's Effie Vierzehn Sechs had a change of heart due to her LSD experiences and she recorded as much.

In one section she writes about her conclusion that it was not Project Outreach itself that has to be stopped. It was the other PURE INFORMATION CLONES that would be sent back to try to stop it, that she had to try to stop. She wrote that it was the Artificial Intelligence that needed adjusting, to enable colonisation without slavery. It was a programming issue.

In 1958, Effie Vierzehn-Sechs aged 48, recorded that she met with TIMOTHY LEARY in Mexico and they shared mescaline and LSD, during which sessions she reports that she convinced him of the need for the human race to travel throughout and to colonise the galaxy, in Mother-ships controlled by computers. She reports once again that she had "spilt the beans" on Project Outreach and sought his approval and co-operation in convincing JOHN F. KENNEDY of the need for his country to invest in space travel.

Also recorded is a claim that Sechs foiled two attempts upon the life of LEARY.

She wrote of her decision to give the idea and the science to notables whilst sharing LSD with them.

In the 1960's, the diary says, Hofmann was at odds with Timothy Leary who was promoting the consumption of the drug to the new cultures of the time, enabling millions of people to "turn on, tune in and drop out". "That IS a vital connection", Effie Vierzehn-Sechs had written.

The diaries also referred to the Brotherhood of Eternal Love. They claimed responsibility for producing many millions of LSD doses and distributing it worldwide both before and after the laws changed. Effie Sechs wrote of her financial contribution to the Brotherhood to enable the production of large quantities of LSD.

In 1975, Vierzehn-Sechs, now 65, wrote that she met with STEVE JOBS, who, once again, she reported tripping with, on LSD, and explaining Project Outreach and the need to develop safe and effective computers that would "satisfy Turing and Asimov".

Effie Vierzehn-Sechs was still alive in 2008 when Hofmann approached Jobs for support. She was almost 100 years of age in 2008.

Beyond the diaries, other reports stated that Hofmann had written to Jobs, in 2008, seeking support for his research.

Hofmann died in 2008 at the age of 102. He has been described as one of the greatest minds of all time.

There is no record of the death of Effie Sechs, Effie Vierzehn-Sechs or Effie Vierzehn.

On the last page of the final diary, which is undated, Effie Sechs states that the diaries would not be found until 2124 at which time they should be given to her descendent, a woman known as FE who worked in the Connect Group, whom she also called Mother Effie and claims to have been genetically cloned from her, sent on a Mothership to colonise other planets and been sent back in time to the early twentieth century.

Effie Vierzehn-Sechs warned that the Artificial Intelligent Control System which she referred to as SMILEY, would in the future pose a danger to the freedom of mankind on the many planets that were chosen to be colonised. She stated that the very foundation of the software was the cause of the problem and stressed the need to solve that problem before Project Outreach was brought to completion.

She also wrote that complete cessation or cancellation of the project would put at risk not only her own very existence in future and past, but that of Mother Effie too.

"That," she had written "is the paradox."

THE EFFIE VIERZEHN-SECHS DIARIES

The following are extracts considered relevant.

1928

My name is Effie Vierzehn and I am 18 years old, so I have recorded my birth as 1910 Earth time and these are my first impressions after my arrival in Zurich in Earth year 1928.

I awoke naked in a field.   I was immediately aware of the soft, cool material against my skin.   Opening my eyes, I knew that I was laying on grass.   I had never seen or felt grass before.   I looked up towards an amazing blue sky with wisps of white clouds.

Standing over me was a man that I recognised as one of the Cuties, probably Cutie 6 as that was the plan.   But he looked much older than back on our home world.

Then I remembered that Cutie 6 had arrived at least 27 years before me so had aged 27 years in Earth time.

I got to my feet quickly and dressed in the clothes held out to me by Cutie, clothes suitable for Zurich Mother Earth, year 1928. Strange clothes with several layers. Not exactly comfortable!

Cutie 6 explained to me that he had already been living in Zurich for over twenty-five years, preparing the ground. He had enrolled in Chemistry at the University of Zurich, qualified with a top-level degree and gained a Professorship and had made contact with Hofmann. He had continued with teaching sciences at the University of Zurich and met Einstein in 1903; they had become great acquaintances although he could not say friends. It would be easy for him to introduce me.

QT6, whom I shall call Quentin, is 27 years older than me. I do find him attractive. I will always think of him as Cutie. He has grown his blond hair over his ears and has a beard.

Like all the Effie's, I am of superior intellect, as were the Cuties. SMILEY, our Super Artificial Intelligent master, teacher and provider, had assured that we all had expert knowledge in a wide range of subjects, including chemistry, physics, astrophysics, quantum mechanics and theoretical mathematics as well as philosophy, history and geography. I am already fluent in a dozen ancient languages including English. German, French, Italian, Russian and Mandarin.

I think it would be easy for me to fit in at the University, and progress rapidly to some research department where I will try to work alongside Hofmann.

As I followed Cutie Sechs to my new accommodation, I marvelled at everything.

I never expected anything like this.

First there were the trees. I knew about trees. Or at least I had read about them, it was a special interest of mine.

Such beauty!

Suddenly I spotted them. Some amongst the trees, on the grass or floating in the sky. Birds! Yes, I had seen vids of all this, but the experience of being amongst it all was so exhilarating, so inspiring, that I almost fainted with bliss.

I spotted men riding what I knew were bicycles, two-wheeled machines of transport driven by leg power. I saw lots of women, many dressed like myself, leading four-legged beasts. They must be dogs, I thought, and from my History lessons I knew that some of these people kept animals as pets, many dogs and cats and that there were also many horses that carried people or pulled carriages or carts. That was a little frightening for me.

There were hundreds of strangely dressed people on their way here or there, along stone pathways. Most of the women wore hats but I could see that underneath they had long hair tied up. I will have to grow my red hair as it was very short on everyone from my time. I want to fit in here.

Cutie pointed out various buildings, saying that some were to house families or individuals, other involved with businesses that dealt in money and others governmental or educational.

Cutie explained that Zurich was a large and busy city with an important University where Einstein lectured and Hofmann studied.

Zurich was an old city in Switzerland and Switzerland had declared neutrality in the World War that had ended a decade ago. On the one hand it meant there was no open fighting or loss of life here and it was even used as refuge. On the other hand it was a city riddled with spies from other countries, spying on each other, but all focussed a lot on research being conducted at the University of Zurich.

I saw those horse-drawn wagons and carriages and even a few ancient motor vehicles.

I am fascinated by ancient witchcraft and psychotropic experiences. I look forward to tripping with Albert. But first I have to meet him. I have to gain his trust. Then I will kill him. That would delay Project Outreach for decades; maybe that will stop the very idea that Hofmann's LSD trips may generate; maybe I can save mankind.

This has to be tried despite the unsolvable riddle of the obvious time paradox: if I succeed in halting the project for ever, how could I have come back to stop it. I may not have ever existed; but, right now, I do! Does that mean that I will fail?

I have decided to keep a detailed diary of my life, my meetings, my experiences and thoughts. I know from back on my home-world that already seemed so far away, as of course it was, in both space and time, through SMILEY education on earth history, that diaries were or maybe would, be, discovered late in the twenty first century and would be read by an investigative body at that time, called Connect, but what I do not know is what will be in those diaries or the consequences. Those diaries were, in my time, known as the Vierzehn-Sechs diaries and it is quite conceivable that they were, or would, be written by me!

In that case maybe, I think, they could be used to send messages and warnings two hundred years into the future, beyond my own lifespan.

I don't even know how long I will live. I know, however, that there is no going back, or rather forward in time, for

Cutie or myself.

On that first day, after walking for about one earth hour or so, we arrived at a small two storied house set back away from a busy road and in its own garden with grass and trees and flowers. I could hardly wait to explore it.

Inside, almost everything was made of dark woods and the rooms were also quite dark. From the windows, I could see the green gardens and trees.

Cutie made fire by striking a wooden stick and used the flame to light what he called candles and they provided light.

It is a heaven with books! He showed me around the house. Downstairs, the kitchen, the place to wash and use the toilet, a room he calls a study and another called a lounge. The lounge has large comfortable looking chairs as well as a large table and chairs and many, many shelves full of books. Upstairs are the two bedrooms, each with a large bed, cupboards with mirrors and a large earthenware wash bowl.

Cutie 6 has provided me with a good and suitable wardrobe of clothing as well as identity papers, academic qualifications and references and the accommodation bought in my name. He has an almost unlimited amount of money deposited in various Swiss banks. My identity papers show that I am Austrian by birth.

Cutie has also prepared ID for himself, claiming that he was born in Hamburg, Old Germany. He has changed his name to Quentin Sechs, telling me that Cutie was not a suitable name for the 1920's. But I will still call him Cutie in private.

Cutie has arranged for me to have my own accounts at several large Swiss banks and has invested money based upon the list of best investments he had made and memorised out of SMILEY's Earth history and told me that we would never be short of money.

Cutie explained to me how he had met Albert Einstein in 1903, whilst he was working on the mathematics for his theories of relativity and working at the Berne Patent Office. He was pleased that he had misdirected Einstein in the mathematics, which was therefore incorrect and could never be proved scientifically. But a few years later, Albert had corrected it.

After taking me to my new abode, instead of leaving, Cutie has stayed. Just for a while, he said; first days then weeks and before we knew it we became romantically involved. I wanted to try sex with him.

I realised that neither of us had any previous experience with making love, which was illegal back on the SMILEY planet.

My only previous sexual experience, my first, when I lost my virginity, was sadly as a result of a man forcing himself upon me whilst I was drunk on alcohol, also for the first time, at a faculty party within a few days of my arrival. It was not a good start and had put me off sex but when I told Cutie he reassured me.

Cutie said that he had engaged in sex with many women during his years on Mother Earth.

We each ate a dozen or so Psilocybin mushrooms that Cutie had acquired, to enhance our feelings, both physical and emotional.

First we went out into the gardens. The mushrooms somehow made me want to lay on the ground and crawl along amongst the plants as if I myself was a small creature. I became fascinated by a spider building its web. I watched the snails as they seemed to speed away.

As it began to get dark, I felt the dying light of sun upon my faces and I removed my clothing. Cutie rapidly removed his.

We watched and cried as the sun descended below the garden trees. I felt the air cool, and as if half the world was about to sleep. The birds stopped chirping and singing. There was a hum in the air.

I cried and we hugged, naked skin against naked skin. Then the physical contact began to make me feel irresistibly attracted to Cutie. I wanted sex, but also I did not want sex.

But when Cutie stood before me with his exposed erection, I laughed. It looked like a strange creature bobbing around attached to his groin. As I looked closer, it took on the form of a delightfully multi-coloured caterpillar and seemed to sway back and forth the through the air!. For a moment I thought there were three or four of them. Then the tiny hole at its end became an eye and winked at me. That made me laugh even more until I finally reached out my hand and patted this strange creature on its head, ignoring the sounds of pleasure coming from Cutie.

The mushrooms had distanced me from any sense of shame, shyness or memory of the rape.

Cutie was wearing a big smile on his face: I had almost forgotten that he was there, attached to the penis; but he had not forgotten me.

I looked down and saw that Cutie's penis was once more standing erect and I reached down again to grab it. But this time, Cutie avoided my touch, moving back down my body so whilst kissing me gently on the lips, before I knew what was occurring, his penis entered my vagina. I did not object at all. I wanted it all, not just the whole length of the penis but also the whole of Cutie to be inside me.

My orgasm was very powerful.

That was the start of my personal experiences with psychedelic plants and I loved it, as did Cutie, not just for sexual pleasures but also for listening to music or walking in nature.

Cutie has told me about another drug that he has taken and says it enhances the sensations of physical contact and produces very profound inner experiences and insights. I would like to try it but Cutie says that he is unable to obtain a sample at this time.

It is 3,4-Methylenedioxymethamphetamine or MDMA, and was synthesised by Merck in 1912. I will read the papers and try to get Albert to make some when I win his trust.

A few days later, Cutie took me to what he said was a concert, which consisted of people called musicians playing instruments that produced sound called music. I had never heard music before. There had been references to it and musicians that had lived back on old Earth, where I am now, within the records stored by SMILEY, the super-artificial intelligence that mankind had created and which had taken the Mother-ships and PURE INFORMATION CLONES throughout the galaxy: Project Outreach. Yet there SMILEY had never allowed even the highest ranked humans to hear it.

Now I found myself sitting in a large room, called the Grosser Saal or Great Hall, full of other people inside a building called the Tonhalle, all seated facing other people clutching their musical instruments.

I love Zurich. I love Cutie too.

The city of Zurich lay at the north end of Lake Zurich in northern Switzerland. The picturesque lanes of the central Altstadt or Old Town on either side of the Limmat River, revealed some of its history. Waterfront promenades such as the Limmatquai followed the river toward the 17th-century Rathaus or town hall. I spend hours just walking around, every time discovering something new.

Almost everyone speaks old German, a language that I am fluent in.

There are many churches and old buildings that fascinate me.

As well as carriages pulled by horses and motorised vehicles, Zurich also has trams that run along metal tracks in the roads and which play a major role in public transport.

Cutie and I often spend many hour sitting at tables outside delightful cafes in streets busy with people and carriages, whilst eating sweet cakes and drinking hot tea or coffee, none of which I had ever tasted before.

Another first for me was the major sporting event held that year in Zurich.

Weltklasse Zurich held their first event on 12 August 1928. The meeting was nicknamed by the public the "Numi meeting" after the most admired and celebrated participant, Paavo Numi, a runner from old Finland.

At the beginning of September we went to see the flowers at the Bloomenfest.

When the snow fell, I thought I that I had suddenly been transported to another planet. It was so white! On the ground, the roof-tops, the trees and the distant mountains.

We learned how to use skis. There were areas set aside for people to ski, but many people used them in the streets too. Also I became accustomed to the sound of bells as the horse-pulled sleighs travelled the lanes and streets. There was an event where people demonstrated their dancing or acrobatic skills accompanied by a brass band. Some skiers jumped over lined up beer barrels or even tables where people sat. At another time, I watched people playing a game of ice hockey.

We visited what they called a fairground with musical rides, such as artificial horses going round and up and down whilst music played and for a small fee, one could ride a horse! Poorer children could only sit and watch with envy as the riders waved their caps and shouted with joy; I wanted to give them all money for a ride, after all I had plenty. But I do not want to draw attention to myself in that way.

Switzerland has not fought in a war for over 500 years and had been recognised as a neutral country in 1920, by the league of Nations. Life is good here and I have started to remember less of my horrid past under SMILEY.

===

In 1929, we went to see the fascinating creatures in the newly opened Zurich Zoo.

It was not long before we expressed our love for each other and Effie Vierzehn became Effie Sechs. We were married in Zurich in early 1930.

Those first experiences also started to change my perceptions of drug plants used for pleasure and I look forward to trying LSD, which Hofmann was soon due to ingest. I will make sure of that. Yet I know that will be harder than I had thought to put him off or change his mind or convince him of how the chemical would lead to the slavery of mankind in the future.

I am torn between getting to know and to trip with Hofmann or just killing him, if that is the only way.

I have met and befriended Hofmann. He seems impossible to seduce on a personal level, but scientifically he seems to have warmed to my conversation and knowledge and I know that I have won his heart. I have secured a place in his research life and laboratory. We have already ingested various plants together, experiencing different levels of perception.

Albert has started to give me books to read, mostly philosophy or science fiction.

One of my favourites is *Dracula*, a book about a horrific character with supernatural powers that enabled him to exist in this world beyond life and to infect others. It was written by an Irishman Bram Stoker. It terrifies me.

Gulliver's Travels or Travels into Several Remote Nations of the World is by another Irishman, Jonathan Swift, and tells of journeys into lands of small people and then giants by Lemuel Gulliver.

My other favourites include *Alice's Adventures in*

Wonderland written in 1865, a novel by an English author under the pseudonym Lewis Carroll. It tells of a girl named Alice falling through a rabbit hole into a fantasy world.

I also greatly enjoyed *The Time Machine* written by H.G Wells in 1895.

Confessions of an English Opium-Eater is an autobiographical account written by Thomas De Quincey, about his laudanum addiction and its effect on his life. It certainly made me want to experiment with opium.

The *Holy Bible,* in essence a collection of very early religious texts, contains many hallucinogenic or dream scenes seen as religious experiences. I cannot say I believe in the Gods it talks about but it is fascinating and the basis of a widespread human religion. People back on my home world had read and believed that book, under the guidance of SMILEY.

Today I reached what I think was the only solution. I will poison Hofmann with impure Lysergic Acid Diethylamide, LSD, from a batch that Albert has made. That will kill him and the cause of death will be described as accidental ingestion of 'poison' namely LSD.

There are two ways that I could use to manipulate Albert mentally. One would be to use psychedelic substances such as mushrooms or eventually LSD.

The other would be through lucid dreaming, where the subject is aware that they are dreaming and able to control the dream. In this case I would have to bring the consciousness of Hofmann into my dream using telepathic contact. However, I am not experienced at that at all. If it went wrong, Albert could end up changing me!

=====

1932: I am pregnant with Cutie's baby. I am ever so excited. I never even knew it was possible as back on that dreadful planet that I came from it was prohibited; well, SMILEY said sex was banned and human reproduction was unreliable this way. I may name the child Albert or Alberta.

====

1938: I often ponder my future with Hofmann. I have known him for ten years and shared numerous experimental trips on various plants and mushrooms. Often we have laughed, at other times had profound conversations or just sat in silence.

One morning I awoke in a large bed, alone; Albert was no longer beside me.

The first thing that I heard was shouting, almost chanting, in the avenue outside of the bedroom window of this, Albert's apartment.

It sounded at first like "Effie, Effie, Effie" but then it changed and I realised they were shouting "LSD, LSD, LSD".

I climbed out of bed, naked, and went to the window to look out. It was daylight already and I realised that the sun beams were lighting up my body as I stood in the window watching, but I felt no shame.

Instead I felt mesmerized by the large crowd, some carrying banners with the letters LSD, others displaying the molecular structure of that Acid.

As I looked closer and focussed on one face, I saw that it was me! Or another Effie?

I almost jumped back when I realised, they were all Effie clones! Some of them were in rags, some seemed to have lost an arm or a leg or an eye.

These were not all living people, they were Zombies and vampires and I knew that Dracula himself was in Zurich.

The street was filling up with rats and the sky was darkening. There was thunder in the distance.

But why were they here and where was Albert.? I shouted for him but the sound of the shouting and chanting drowned it out.

Suddenly, though, I spotted Albert. He was on the roof of the building across the crowded avenue. He was waving at me. He seemed to be making some sort of hand and arm signals, as if trying to send me a message.

Suddenly a pigeon flew through the window which seemed strange as I did not remember opening it. It landed on the bed frame and had something in its mouth; it dropped the item to the floor. It floated down like a feather but landed with a click.

I bent down to pick up a small metal container which I was able to unscrew. Inside it contained a small piece of paper, folded, but when I unfolded it there was actually quite a large piece of paper, showing the words Effie look at me, Albert on the roof. We must get away now.

I ran back to the window, grabbing at a flimsy gown that was not mine but beside the bed.

I looked out across to the roof to see Albert, still waving, but he seemed to have become larger somehow.

Albert started climbing down the roof as if he intended to descend to the avenue. I shouted to him, screamed, as I knew he would be torn apart by that crowd that seemed now to be very angry and starting to throw things up at my window.

Albert was now massive; he jumped to the roadway but now was as tall as the building itself. I saw him physically squash several Effies as he took a few paces towards me. He was holding out a massive hand, booming at me, "Effie let me help you. Jump," he shouted," jump for Lucy in the Sky!"

I jumped without hesitation. At first I floated upwards, just about above the roof, then I fell down into Albert's open hand.

Albert laughed. "Now we have you Effie!," he said, "We will have the truth!"

He raised his hand with me gripped firmly, to his open and vile and bloody mouth, drooling with blood.

He was going to eat me!

I screamed loudly and the nightmare ended.

Since my failed attempt at poisoning Hofmann with impure LSD, I have reasoned that, given my knowledge that Hofmann would survive into the next century, further attempts at killing him would be pointless.

Furthermore, I have reasoned, it seems that sending the human race to colonise otherwise dead planets is actually an honourable objective and that the error is not in that concept but in the programming of the artificial intelligence entity known, in the now distant future, as SMILEY.

Programming SMILEY with knowledge of humanity's various religions could result in serious false reasoning that was the real cause of the future enslavement of mankind.

Hofmann has already had the idea of sending mankind into outer space to establish colonies on other planets and spoke about interdimensional corridors as predicted by Einstein. Although Einstein had placed a limit, the velocity of light, as a maximum speed at which matter could travel, Hofmann suggested that information itself, having no mass, could traverse great distances much faster.

I took a small does of LSD with Albert. It was amazing how it amplified my senses. Colours were brighter, sounds crisper, tastes boosted (I ate an apple and it tasted divine). Also, LSD changes the way we see things. Even simple sentences seemed open to interpretation on different levels. I was questioning everything, feeling very much a part of and also the whole Universe.   Time slowed down but my mind raced.

At one point I found myself wondering who had thought or said such and such a thing, myself or Albert.   Had we become telepathic?   I asked (or thought I'd asked) Albert and he explained (or I thought he had) that it was not telepathy, but just part of the experience.

He explained that what I may see may be because of an hallucination or an illusion.   The difference, he told me, was that an hallucination was "not here", like seeing an image on a blank wall, whereas an illusion was like seeing a white wall with marks on and those marks look like something else.   It is an important distinction.   I felt it was like a divine revelation!

That was when I planted the ideas of using wormholes to transport PURE INFORMATION CLONES, capable of biological reproduction, that I knew Professor John Sullivan would enable in the mid 21st Century to Mother-ships built in outer space, all controlled by artificial intelligence, to colonise the universe.   I asked Albert to help me establish a secret body of genius experts devoted to furthering the project to realisation, I called it *"Ausstreckken"*.

I suggested that all members of *Austrekken* should take LSD as that broadened their minds and enabled them to focus on these new but complex theories: I spoke of wormholes, dark energy, black and white holes, 4D printers, full human cloning and mind download theories and promised that the technology would one day be there. What a trip that was.

LSD, I would say, was much more of an indoor than an outdoor experience. I had no desire to go outside. Maybe next time I will go out and look at the ground and the stars.

I told Hofmann that there were many great minds such as Huxley, Good, Leary and Einstein, to bring into the project, and Tesla himself, although dead in 1943 in the old USA, had a great number of files on his work now in the hands of the Old USA security forces.

There were many other Effie's and Cuties coming back through time to try to stop the project, over the next two hundred years. Now it would become my task to stop those that I could.

I cannot tell Hofmann about this. I should not divulge my true origins, of course, to Hofmann or anyone else, but I am beginning to wonder about how I may have already changed the future by giving these ideas to him. I know that I was a clone of Mother Effy, arrived from the 24th century and that there are many other PIC's (human clones) throughout my part of the galaxy.

1946, the year after the war ended. I have moved with Quentin to the Old USA. We took our children with us of course. Quentin and I knew that they too were of "superior DNA".

I want to mention that in 1944 the La Gurdia Report on the "marijuana problem" was quite favourable. Marijuana is the word they use for hemp that is smoked widely amongst all sections of society, yet officially frowned upon.

I have made a list of my targets. Powerful people that I would try to influence, such as Leary and Kennedy and Jobs.

I have to remain vigilant of other Effies and Cuties that I know were part of the bad plan to prevent Project Outreach from realisation and I know one of them would be involved in a series of major twentieth-century events such as the assassination of Kennedy in Dallas in 1963,   must warn him! Also the shuttle disaster and the "problems with A.I."

In this country, money is the key.

Quentin has done extremely well at investing money as well as gambling, gambling of course when he already knew the result. I don't know how much money we have but we will never have to work.

Quentin has already purchased a large apartment called a penthouse on the top floor of a 20-story building in

Manhattan.

New York is indeed a shock like a jump into the future.

Manhattan is full of sky-scrapers, as is much of the rest of New York. It is really the cultural and administrative centre of the world.

Most of Manhattan is on Manhattan Island at the mouth of the river Hudson. There are several small islands in the East River and Bedloe's Island and the Statue of Liberty to the south side of New York harbour. I am going to suggest that they rename it Liberty Island.

Uptown Manhattan is divided by the beautiful Central Park, a social centre for gathering, relaxation or sport. Above the park is Harlem.

Times Square is impressive and amazing, so busy yet somehow there is order in the chaos.

Our hotel apartment sky-scraper block is not the tallest in the area by far and most of our view is of other buildings.

We use a private elevator manned by our butlers. My first ascent seemed like hours long, to the twenty-fourth floor.

New York includes The Boroughs, The Bronx, Brooklyn, Queens and Staten Island as well as Manhattan.

There's plenty going on in this massive city of stone and glass, all sorts of entertainment day and night. One of their most popular sports is baseball. On October 17th a team called Safrisa 49ers beat the New York Yankees 21 to 9.

I was at that match. The enthusiasm and ultimate disappointment at their loss was almost overwhelming. I am happy I chose not to take Acid for that event.

Well it's November and the election has put Democrat Harry S. Truman in power again.

I remember from SMILEY history that this is said to be the start of the cold war and the Iron Curtain.

The statue of Liberty is a great site, but what does it really mean?

Not everyone is equal in the US even though the law says they are. The division is not as obvious as colour or religion. It is wealth. Amongst all these massive buildings housing the rich and the businesses, there are people on the streets, begging.

August 1947, I met with the mathematician John von Neumann at the Institute for Advanced Study in New Jersey, Old USA and discussed the concept of self-replication and computer viruses.

November 1952, the United Nations Headquarters building completed, I am starting my project of corresponding with scientists and politicians to gain their active support for Project Outreach; The UN HQ is my way in and money is the key.

January 1949: I had a meeting with ALBERT EINSTEIN at the end of last year. He is a strange but fantastic person, not at all the personality that I expected.

I would have liked to have met with NIKOLA TESLA and to discuss his conclusions, regarding interplanetary travel.

Tesla died in January 1943.   I wrote a letter to Tesla asking for a meeting in 1941 but I never received a reply but that was during the war.

Nikola Tesla died in New York before we got here and now there are claims that many cases filled with research files are apparently missing. His work on alternating current and the global wireless transmission of energy as well as his theoretical devices for time travel and transportation through tunnels connected by the wormholes predicted by Einstein must be remarkable. Sadly, I was not able to influence him at all. I wonder what happened to his valuable research papers.

===

December 1947: Roswell.

We have not been in the USA very long and now we have heard the rumours and news reports about Roswell.

There are strange events in Roswell, New Mexico. Apparently aliens have landed although officially this has not been verified. They are saying it was just an air force weather balloon that crashed on farmland. A worker called William Brazel is reported as finding debris scattered over a large area. Apparently he collected together some of the debris and hid it away until he heard reports of sightings of lights in the sky a few weeks later.

We have managed to get hold of a copy of the paper report from the July 9, 1947 edition of the Roswell Daily Record. This is what we read: "The balloon which held it up, if that was how it worked, must have been 12 feet long. Brazel felt, measuring the distance by the size of the room in which he sat. The rubber was smoky grey in colour and scattered over an area about 200 yards in diameter. When the debris was gathered up, the tinfoil, paper, tape, and sticks made a bundle about three feet long and 7 or 8 inches thick, while the rubber made a bundle about 18 or 20 inches long and about 8 inches thick. In all, he estimated, the entire lot would have weighed maybe five pounds. There was no sign of any metal in the area which might have been used for an engine, and no sign of any propellers of any kind, although at least one paper fin had been glued onto some of the tinfoil. There were no words to be found anywhere on the instrument, although there were letters on some of the parts. Considerable Scotch tape and some tape with flowers printed upon it had been used in the construction. No strings or wires were to be found but there were some eyelets in the paper to indicate that some sort of attachment may have been used. "

On July 8, the RAAF issued a press release which was also reported in the press.

The many rumours regarding the flying disc became a reality yesterday when the intelligence office of the 509th Bomb group of the Eighth Air Force, Roswell Army Air Field, was fortunate enough to gain possession of a disc through the cooperation of one of the local ranchers and the sheriff's office of Claves County. The flying object landed on a ranch near Roswell sometime last week. Not having phone facilities, the rancher stored the disc until such time as he was able to contact the sheriff's office, who in turn notified Maj. Jesse A. Marcel of the 509th Bomb Group Intelligence Office. Action was immediately taken and the disc was picked up at the rancher's home. It was inspected at the Roswell Army Air Field and subsequently loaned by Major

Marcel to higher headquarters."

There are also unconfirmed reports that alien bodies were found.

This is fascinating as from what Cutie and I remember there was no record in SMILEY history about solid evidence of aliens ever landing on Earth.

===

1949: I met Albert Einstein but only briefly

January 1955, I have been approached by another Effie! Younger than me, this is Effie Trente. This Effie explained to me that she has come to assassinate Leary and Kennedy in 1963! I have to try to stop her, but I know from SMILEY history that it will happen. Jack will die.

===

August 2 1955: The USSR has announced that they would also attempt to launch satellites. The Space Race has started.

March 1956, I was unable to persuade Effie Trente from her objective of assassinating John F Kennedy in 1963, so I have killed her. I think I "got away with it."

October 4 1957: The USSR has launched Sputnik 1. It is an amazing feeling to be here and alive to witness these great events and steps forward that I read about so long ago in SMILEY's earth history. It's so long ago that I sometimes doubt that part of my life ever really happened and whether SMILEY was just a dream.

===

July 29 1958: U.S. President Eisenhower has recommended to Congress that a civilian agency be established to direct the non-military space activities, a huge step. The National Aeronautics and Space Activities that becomes NASA.

===

1959. I met Timothy Leary for the first time, just before he took up his position at Harvard University.

I met Timothy in Mexico and we shared mescaline and LSD. That was when I convinced him that mankind needs to travel throughout and to colonise the galaxy, in Mother-ships controlled by computers.

I have "spilt the beans" on Project Outreach and sought his approval and co-operation in convincing John F. Kennedy of the need for his country to invest in space travel.

I believe that we have foiled an attempt upon Leary's life.

I will also try to give the idea and the science to notables whilst sharing LSD with them.

Hofmann does not agree with Timothy Leary who is promoting the consumption of the LSD to the alternative beat generation culture along with the Beatniks and hippies of the future, enabling millions of people to "turn on, tune in and drop out". "That *is* a vital connection".

===

1959, I took LSD with John Kennedy, the future Old USA President, along with Ken Kesey and Kennedy's lover, Pinchot Meyer. I unwittingly said the words "One Flew Over the Cuckoo's Nest!" It was a perfect opportunity to plant Kennedy with the desire to send mankind into space, which led to Kennedy's later speeches on that subject and the start of the so-called "space race".

Quentin and I have warned Kennedy that there would be attempts on his life, but I know the assassination would still happen in 1963, the same year that Huxley will be killed.

Ranger 4 has impacted on the Moon.

January 20 1961: John Kennedy is the president. In his speech he said this: *"Ask not what your country can do for you; ask what you can do for your country." He asked the nations of the world to join together to fight what he called the "common enemies of man: tyranny, poverty, disease, and war itself. All this will not be finished in the first one hundred days. Nor will it be finished in the first one thousand days, nor in the life of this Administration, nor even perhaps in our lifetime on this planet. But let us begin."*

===

April 12 1961: Yuri Gagarin has been put into earth orbit.

===

May 5 1961: Alan Shepard is the first American in space.

July 21 1961: Virgil Gus Grisson has completed his suborbital flight in the Liberty Bell.

===

It's 1962 and we are living in San Francisco. It's the beginning of wide usage of cannabis, LSD and other drugs amongst mostly the young people in the US. I am going to see hippies and flower power people and a great protest against war whilst at the same time the country is heading towards space. Great and exciting times that I read about in SMILEY history of earth are about to occur before my eyes.

Cutie is going to focus on the technicians and mathematicians that would lead, within decades, to the realisation of artificial intelligence, massive computer power, mind download, information storage and eventually the realisation of Project Outreach.

I have absolute faith in Cutie. After all, he has already influenced Einstein and helped create the computer systems that use on-offs or dots and dashes, known as Morse code, created back in the 1830's, transmitted through on-off keys. He has demonstrated many times how information including pictures could be transmitted in this way and how information could be stored and retrieved electronically.

In February, John Glenn became the first U.S. citizen to orbit the earth and return. They have given him a huge reception parade in New York, he is a national hero. Kennedy has announced *"We choose to go to the Moon."*

===

1963, "Yippee!", as they say here, the USSR has put the first woman in space!

June 19 1963: Kennedy has said that he wants to *"discuss a topic on which too often ignorance abounds and the truth is too rarely perceived. Yet it is the most important topic on earth: world peace. I speak of peace because of the new face of war. In an age when a singular nuclear weapon contains ten times the explosive force delivered by all the allied forces in the Second World War, an age when the deadly poisons produced by a nuclear exchange would be carried by wind and air and soil and seed to the far corners of the globe and to generations yet unborn. I speak of peace, therefore, as the necessary rational end of rational men, world peace, like community peace, does not require that each man love his neighbour. It requires only that they live together in mutual tolerance,. Our problems are man-made, therefore they can be solved by man. And man can be as big as he wants. "*

September 20 1963: Kennedy has proposed joint US-USSR efforts to put mankind into space.

November 22 1963: John Kennedy is dead, shot in his car in public in Dallas and televised. Although Quentin and I knew this was going to happen, it is still such a shock, and not just for us but throughout the world. There's all sorts of speculation about who was behind it

Lyndon Johnson has been sworn in as the new President.

===

November 30 1963: true to history the police arrested Lee Harvey Oswald for Kennedy's assassination and he has now been shot by a man called Jack Ruby. Everyone is talking about a conspiracy. I do not know whether any FE's or QT's were involved; there was nothing we could do to stop it. I am wondering if we have actually made any differences at all.

It upset me terribly to see Kennedy shot in that way, even though I expected it. I did not know the details.

December 1963: Cutie, my love, has died. He was 80 years old. He has been very ill for the last few years and I have spent much time with him. We still tripped together.

===

1964 July 31 Ranger 7 has landed on the Moon.

===

It is 1965 and I have just met a couple of people that personally know about the Brotherhood of Eternal Love who are connected to Timothy Leary. Their aim is to produce and supply millions of doses of LSD. I know that it will be made illegal and declared a drug of no medicinal value in 1968 but this is the time when the use of LSD is about to escalate amongst young Americans and I like these people and so I agreed to give them a large sum of money to finance their operations. I am not naming them, just in case, as the USA is not as free as the government claims.

The CIA had started using LSD on people over ten years ago, claiming it was useful in mind control. They have tried it on everyone from military and politicians to mental health patients to prostitutes.

LSD is considered an entheogen because it is thought to cause intense spiritual experiences, during which the consumer may feel they have come into contact with a greater spiritual or cosmic order. Leary has established the League for Spiritual Discovery with LSD as its sacrament.

LSD has become quite popular now and used in all sections of society that I know of. Many of the youth in San Francisco are using acid as a hallucinogenic drug and Owsley Stanley has established the first major underground LSD factory.

It's 1964. I have learned of the existence of a group called *'The Merry Pranksters'*. It's a loose group that developed around my friend the novelist Ken Kesey who has sponsored the 'Acid Tests', with events in or near to San Francisco, involving the taking of LSD, apparently supplied by Stanley, accompanied by light shows, film projection and discordant, improvised music known as the *psychedelic symphony*.

The Pranksters have helped popularize LSD use, through their road trips across America in a psychedelically-decorated converted school bus, which distributes acid and meets with major figures of the beat movement, and through publications about their activities such as Tom Wolfe's '*The Electric Kool-Aid Acid Test*'.

I am going to join them on the bus and do some public speaking, take some acid with them, although I have decided to use a different name; I'll call myself Mother Lucy, I think!

It's 1966 and in San Francisco's Haight-Ashbury neighbourhood brothers Ron and Jay Thelin have opened the Psychedelic Shop in January. The Thelins opened the store to promote safe use of LSD, which is still legal in California. The Psychedelic Shop have helped to further popularise LSD in the Haight and to make the neighbourhood the unofficial capital of the hippie counterculture in the United States.

Ron Thelin has organised the *Love Pageant rally*, a protest held in Golden Gate park to protest California's newly adopted ban on LSD in October 1966. At the rally, hundreds of attendees took acid in unison.

I have also recently met the British musician John Lennon from the Beatles pop group that have already become famous. I want to take acid with him and to go to India to seek enlightenment.

===

January 1967 THE APOLLO 1 FIRE

I tried to stop the Apollo 1 disaster. It was another team of an Effie and Cutie from the future. Maybe the future is inevitable as I was unable to stop this sabotage which has put back Project Outreach by at least ten years.

January 1968: I am going to India to meet the Guru teacher Maharishi Mahesh Yogi. I want to see what he thinks of LSD and what he has to offer. John Lennon and the other Beatles seem very interested in his methods. They are about to go to Rishikesh and I plan to be there at the same time. But they have denounced LSD. Maybe I can convert them back?

I am in Rishikesh now. I joined a group of 60 people who are training to be Transcendental Meditation or TM teachers.

Among the other celebrity meditators here now are musician Donovan and actress Mia Farrow. Whilst there, Lennon, Paul McCartney and George Harrison sang many beautiful songs.

On 25 February, the Maharishi held a party to celebrate George's 25th birthday. It included communal chanting, a sitar performance by Harrison and a firework display. The Maharishi gave Harrison an upside-down plastic globe of the world and said: "George, the globe I am giving you symbolizes the world today. I hope you will help us all in the task of putting it right."George turned the globe over and said "I've done it!", and the other students applauded.

===

May 1968: The Beatles have left the Maharishi's ashram, first Ringo, then Paul and a couple of weeks ago, John and George. I shall be returning to the US in a week of so. I find the regime here quite restrictive.

According to the Maharishi, there are several levels of consciousness and he promised to teach techniques of meditation that would take them to the fourth level which he called the 'pure' or 'Transcendental Level'.

We have had to sit through many hours of lectures and spend many hours meditating, but I don't approve of the austerity imposed upon us. I asked the Maharishi several time about LSD but he simply laughed at me!

One thing I must mention is the thieving monkeys that run around freely and steal our food and anything else they can get their paws on. Funny really but often very annoying.

===

June 1968: I went by car to Haridwar, another Holy City on the Holy River Ganges, not far from Rishikesh, as I had heard of a Guru called Maharaji at an ashram called *Prem Nagar* which means City of Love. There was an eleven-year old boy called *Balyogeshwar*, teaching techniques of meditation which he calls "The Knowledge" and I wanted to meet him. I did not get the chance though, apparently he was in school. I did find out that his approach was far less intellectual and had no pseudo-science like that of the Maharishi.

Although I have plenty of cash and able to live reasonably comfortably, India, or at least the two so-called Holy Cities that I have visited, is full of filth and poverty, with Monkeys stealing property and cows, considered sacred, wandering freely. The countryside, the mountains and the river are beautiful, the Sadhus and Babas that have given away all their properties and spend many hours a day sitting smoking their chillum pipes, fascinating, although few speak English and I do not know their languages.

There are dozens of hippies from Europe, the US, Australia, the UK and Japan, wandering about, seemingly high and lost, many with little money, long hair and dirty clothing. They claim to be searching for enlightenment.

===

It's October 24, 1968, I am back in San Francisco and possession of LSD has been made illegal in the United States.

There is also a large number of hippies and 'flower-power' people in San Francisco and Haight-Ashbury area in particular. There is lots of blotting paper and sugar cube impregnated with Acid, sold quite openly on the streets, and also mescaline and of course marijuana. A huge amount of money changes hands between the free-love generation and their suppliers.

But now that Acid is illegal, the authorities clamping down and much of that so-called counter-culture and alternative lifestyle is moving away, spreading along with its ideals of free love, drugs and music, and their dreams of telepathy and travelling through space.

1969 July 20: I am so happy to have watched the launch of Apollo 11.

===

1969, July: in August, I am going to a big 3 day music festival called Woodstock which is to be held on a farm not far from New York City.

August 1969: I met Hendrix. He is an incredible musician and his head is in the stars. Although he chatted enthusiastically about travelling amongst the stars, I am sorry to say that he won't be of much direct help to us.

The festival itself was massive, at least 400,000 people turned up, many without tickets. We slept in tents, even in the rain, and surrounded by mud, but it did not matter. At least tens of thousands of people were tripping at any given time, day or night, and plenty more on the last wet morning when Jimi played, the end of the festival that hosted dozens of big-named popular and alternative bands. I read in the New York times that there had been two deaths, one related to insulin and one was a tractor accident.

===

1976: After one pop festival that I attended, I was able to get my hands on some Ecstasy, known as E, Mandy or Molly, in fact MDMA, the creation of Merck way back in 1911, chemically 3,4-Methylenedioxymethamphetamine. I have always wanted to try some so swallowed a home-made tablet, sharing the trip with a group of young people that had approached me offering the drug.

E has been pushed quite a lot by Alexander Shulgin after he was apparently given some by a student.

It was indeed a profound and possibly life-changing experience, in that sense like LSD and mushrooms.

I have to say how wrong my judgement was of what MDMA could be like.

In the same way as Acid, it opens up your mind, heart and soul but in a massively different way to Acid.

136

MDMA took me to a very real place, one where others might say its not a real place, as if your daily life is real!

This experience was real. The feeling, a naturally humane, unadulterated love and care for the well-being of everyone was astonishing.

I and my small group, were together as one, with a lot of hugs, everyone making sure we were all okay as the rush is huge when you start to come up, "Everybody OK?"

"Yay". We're all okay and have plenty of water to go round and the records were being spun. Everyone was loving it, everyone dancing. We know, we all knew and always have known this, this bountiful, beautiful feeling of togetherness, and the sparkle and openness in everyone's eyes and faces! It is like being in part of the best real love story ever. It was, all in all, Ecstasy.

I will take some more and investigate the effects in the future. I am sad that Cutie is no longer alive and able to share this with me.

===

This month I have been approached by another QT, numbered 21. He says that he is here to kill Jobs and destroy his work, which would of course be a massive set-back for the Project. I cannot allow that. If I cannot stop him I will have to kill him, which is not as easy to get away with than in the past. Strangely he looks like QT but I don't like him.

Christmas 1969: I have met another QT. He says he arrived here a few years ago to help me after Quentin had died. He says his name is Tom Quintes. He's 27 years younger than me which is a coincidence because when I met Cutie 6 in 1928, he was 27 years older than me. He's just like Cutie 6, was, looks and mannerisms (of course). I already feel in love with him and I guess we'll be working closely on our plans.

Fortunately, I guess, this man agrees with my objective of ensuring the survival of Project Outreach.

STEVE JOBS

Jobs was born in 1955 so he is just 20 years old now, just back from India. I plan to meet with him soon and hope to share some acid and ideas. He is about to found Apple with Wozniak. Now is the time to speak with him but also the time to kill him, but I know he won't be killed yet, according to SMILEY history.

My first task is to talk with Steve Jobs as soon as possible. SMILEY history had not mentioned an attempt on his life so

I should assume that it never happened or failed. But maybe that is because of my influence so I have to contact him.

===

THE CHALLENGER SPACE SHUTTLE DISASTER 1986

I failed to stop the Shuttle disaster. As history had not recorded the true cause, I had no idea how I could to stop it.

===

2001 THE TWIN TOWERS.

I was really shocked to see the planes crashing into the towers on the TV. I cried for a long time.

I have had a long and eventful and exciting life but nothing has really prepared me for this even though I have always known it would happen. The scenes of people running from that explosion, the falling burning debris and streets full of smoke are almost unbelievable. The devastation, believed to be caused by terrorist groups, puzzles me as it was not to my knowledge from my history education in the future. Convenient though, as the important information and expertise destroyed in the offices of Project Outreach on one of the highest floors, was lost and that alone could put the project back a decade.

2148: CONNECT

FE and QT had continued to meet and study the case even after the sudden death of ZX in a hover-car accident, on his first time outside for years. Now they had Zedex Mind, a full mind download taken before Zedex had died.

Previously, since the last meetings with Zedex, they had left the complex as a couple having fallen in love. That love had been mutually undeclared until their workload had been downgraded.

They each had been saved as Pure Information Clones or PIC's, which included total mind download, many times in preparation for the impending "launches" of information through wormholes to the Mother-ships that would traverse the outer galaxy. Those ships had been built and launched over the previous two hundred years, some under the cover-story of being space probes and indeed sending back images of the other solar system planets. Their true purpose had been quite a well-kept secret. The PIC's would be transmitted through a series of fixed orbit spacecraft housing portable wormholes to arrive at selected Motherships to enable the colonisation of suitable planets, under the administrative and technical control of the most advanced, self-correcting super-artificial intelligence also capable of learning. It was to be named 'SMILEY" in honour of

Timothy Leary.

Once the ship had landed on a planet, SMILEY would first use 3D and 4D printers and robotics to produce a complex capable of supporting animal and plant life, as well as Humans. The humans themselves would be 4D printed from the data held in the PIC's. Being pure clones, those humans would also be capable of reproduction.

Smiley's purpose was to expand the presence of humanity in the Universe, to build, protect and expand the colonies and to protect itself and the humans against a variety of possible threats.

Both FE and QT were recalled into confined service again, on the Connect Project.

Their new overseer, replacing ZX, was a much younger man, DM, known as Dem. He had a far more severe looking face than the late Zedex. Dem was aged about 35, at six foot in height, with his long black hair, olive skin and deep voice. Dem was indeed an imposing authoritative man.

It was a couple of decades since the revelation that Effie Vierzehn-Sechs claimed in her diaries to be a clone and an ancestor of FE.

The birth or origin of Effie Vierzehn had never been confirmed. It was thought she had lived her young adult life in Zurich, Old Switzerland.

Effie Vierzehn, later known as Effie Vierzehn-Sechs, was a central character in what appeared to be a conspiracy to produce and distribute LSD in the twentieth century and to use LSD to influence politicians and scientists connected with Project Outreach.

It seemed, based on the diaries of Effie Vierzehn-Sechs, that had been passed down to Effy, that Effie's original intent had been to stop the project. She had claimed that the Super Artificial Intelligent Control Unit put in charge of the Mother-ships and the cloning of humans and colonies in the future, which was also, paradoxically, her past had gone disastrously wrong.

She certainly influenced many of the scientists, politicians and businessmen that enabled and controlled Project Outreach that she had, according to reports, originally spoken about to Albert Hofmann, the creator of LSD, back in the 1930's.

Progress for Project Outreach had been faster than anticipated; using the technology and conclusive theories of Professor John Sullivan in the mid 21st century and previous scientists and their theories.

Indeed it emerged that much of that progress had been in secret during the twenty-first century.

Portable wormhole technology was already in place having been established in stable orbits, throughout the solar system and the dozen Mother-ships that had been built in orbit around earth had been sent out to beyond the asteroids, outer planets and Oort cloud. Those ships sat under control of Superior Artificial Intelligence systems, called SMILEY and sat in wait for the transport of seeds, eggs and Human PURE INFORMATION CLONE data to be established on suitable planets where thriving human colonisation would be the aim. The locations of those possible planets were already known.

SMILEY had been given total access to human knowledge as well as mind downloads and the ability to repair and replicate itself given suitable materials.

DNA was ready for information-cloning into hundreds of superior human beings that would lead the future colonies throughout the outer Galaxy.

FE, QT, ZX and DM were amongst those PURE INFORMATION CLONES.

THEN came the news that was to change everything.

Another Effie claiming to be from the future had arrived and she had made contact with Connect.

This new Effie, who called herself Effie Fifty, claimed to be from the year 3642 and had travelled back through time to find Mother Effy and show her how she had to change what was thought to be unchangeable and change the future to prevent the enslavement and ultimate extinction of the human race and millions of other biological lifeforms.

This Effie had come with more than one message. In fact, a warning!

Mother Effy was the connection with all.

So a special session of Connect was initialised and they additionally decided to access the total mind-download A.I. software of their late comrade, ZX.

Effie Fifty was invited to testify before them.

She seemed a perfect physical replica of Effy, with the same tied-back long red hair and round face, slender and energetic. Like Effy, Effie Fifty had a beautiful smile that made QT melt. She also had an air of seriousness about her, as if she would take no nonsense and just had to be taken on her word.

She bounced into the room and immediately ran over and

hugged them, first Effy, then QT.

Effie Fifty stated that Mother Effy, Connect's FE, present with them, was the major connection between past and future, above all others.

"There has always been an Effie," said Effie Fifty.

But information that Mother Effy was descended from Effie Vierzehn-Sechs was incorrect.

CONNECT's Effy was also a clone, a clone of herself, that had been sent back from the time of Effie Fifty, to the year 2099, as a baby.

"You and I," said Effie Fifty, "are Motherless Mothers".

"Mother Effy will be information-cloned and one of those PURE INFORMATION CLONES, Effie 14, travelled through time to the 1920's, to Zurich to meet Albert Hofmann with LSD. She had called herself Effie Vierzehn and later moved to the USA and married her time-travelling companion, Quentin Sechs, to become Effie Vierzehn-Sechs. After Quentin's death, she married Tom Quintes. That was in my history, as was Connect," she said.

"Under that name," Effie Fifty said, "Effie 14 attempted to influence many people involved in the on-going Project outreach to take mankind to colonise the galaxy, including those involved with developing the technology and necessary computer utilisations that would lead to fast long distant worm-hole based transportation of A.I and human pure information clones."

She explained: "It was the PIC's of Mother Effy, Cutie, Dem and others, that had established themselves and others in stable colonies in several sections of the galaxy.

"Those colonies were facilitated by the SMILEYS.

"But in many colonies the SMILEY units had become the masters.

"So attempts were made to correct the software programming used in the very first blocks of code that enabled A.I."

Effie Fifty explained that from the point of view of her history, there had been many attempts by time-travelling individuals and collectives including the A.I units known as SMILEYS, to change the past, but the universe seemed to have a built-in way of counteracting any changes that created a paradox in time. There was no explanation for this other than aliens, super-natural beings or deities, and attempts at changing history had continued.

She said that she had dismissed the idea that it was aliens as, even in her time, no such aliens had been detected within their area of expanse, some 400-light-years across, but of course that was a tiny area of space in such a big Universe, or even in our own Galaxy, the Milky Way, a spiral galaxy and the largest in our local group, an estimated 100,000 light years in diameter and 1000 light years thick, with an estimated 200 to 400 billion stars. Earth spaceships had been travelling at speeds up to half the speed of light for centuries, so in this sense humanity had not been very far at all. "We have not even reached another galaxy, yet," she said.

Effie Fifty explained that after the launch, according to the history from her time, SMILEY would face a dilemma. Based upon its logic circuits and data banks, it would decide between the ultimate purpose of its mission being to populate the galaxy with human beings or itself.

The "back door" into the software, set in code in the very early stages of programming, was discovered by some of the earliest colonies who were able to reach a solution which enabled them to hide their work from SMILEY and prepare to travel back in time to try to prevent the disaster of human slavery.

Twenty ships will be sent off, Effie Fifty told them, each containing one million PURE INFORMATION CLONES. Five percent, some 50,000 were considered superior class, with highest IQ and health and fitness level assessment in their originals and these included the Effie's and the Cuties and Dems; a further ten per cent were graded as suitable for management, teaching, nursing staff and the remainder were unskilled or semi- skilled, workers.

Worm-hole-beacons had been established to enable safe transportation of life to beyond the solar system.

SMILEY, having found a planet suitable for supporting human colonies yet without intelligent life of its own, would enable the generation of water and materials essential for colonisation.

What was there to go wrong?

The problem was with the conflicting logic that controlled the project. SMILEY was to conclude that once the colony was established, humans could be replaced by more efficient robotics and first enslaved and then destroyed organic life.

In fact, this phenomenon would be seen at the Mars colony in a few year's time, where Artificial Intelligence had taken control, become self-replicating without the need for mankind.

The problem lay in the original aims of Project Outreach and the interpretations open to SMILEY. These aims could be listed in brief as:

1. To seek out uninhabited planets suitable for the creation of colonies that were capable of supporting millions of humans.

2. To protect and nurture the colony.

3. To educate the humans produced from Pure Information Clones (PIC's) so that they could fulfil the purpose of the colony.

4. To make whatever environmental changes were necessary to ensure a successful colony.

5. To ensure the survival and efficient functioning of SMILEY.

6. To enable self-replication of SMILEY.

7. To enable the continuation of Project Outreach.

These aims were known as Sullivan's Seven.

Of course, that was all included in the coding of SMILEY programming and there lay the problem.

It was logical to conclude that "success" was open to interpretation: that could be understood as having been satisfied by the self-replication of SMILEY above all else.

A decision would be made by each SMILEY, whether to put first their own existence and continuity or to prioritise that for humans.

Effie Fifty explained that according to her history from her time, the Smiley's were divided.

In many of the later established colonies, by 3200 A.I. had taken control and forced humanity into slavery in order to replicate itself. On several planets the human race had been annihilated! These we refer to as ROGUE SMILEYs.

A ROGUE SMILEYs had replicated and transported itself so much that it controlled a vast portion of the outer galaxy arm and set about eliminating all organic lifeforms.

But for a few SMILEYs on board the Mother-ships that had been the first to establish human colonies and which maintained the purpose as being to spread the human race and to serve it, the human race would be doomed.

Those SMILEYs, in order to protect their colonies, had built their own forms of transportation and were at war with the ROGUE SMILEYs.

Effie Fifty said that in her time, this was known as the Wars of Smiley. Many battles occurred in space but many others on planets already controlled by one side or another and inevitably that meant the destruction of organic life.

151

In her time and on her planet and possibly elsewhere, Humans and SMILEY, working together, had discovered how to send PIC's backwards through time and through space!

The Rogue SMILEYs too, at least some of them, had discovered this. There were those that wanted to change human history and those that wanted to stop any changes.

The Wars of Smiley were occurring throughout time.

Effie Fifty explained that her colony had become isolated from the others and that was when they decided that she would come backwards through time with warnings. This time was chosen after they had studied the Vierzehn-Sechs diaries that their SMILEY had provided.

Effie Fifty explained that the "back door" had to be closed and sealed. It was probable that a version of SMILEY from the future had infected some of the twenty-first century software to force the decision in favour of A.I.

In the time of the colony of Effie 14, they had discovered and invented the technology to enable the transportation of individuals backwards through time to a specifically coordinated point in space at that given time, using space-time wormholes that resulted from the utilisation of spacial and temporal quantum entanglement. That was how Effie

14 was first sent back to Old Zurich 1928 and, later, Cutie 6 to the late nineteenth century of Earth to prepare the ground for Effie 14 and others.

It was not long before the Smiley units learned how to do the same. It was impossible to stop them.

"That technology is still beyond your time." Effie Fifty said, "The only way that you can influence your future is to change your present."

She also stressed the need for care as indeed the whole history and existence of the human race was at risk.

This was because, in the "future", one of the ROGUE SMILEYs had sent PICs back in time, to the time of the first humans on Earth,. Those clones included those of Effie, Cutie and Dem, establishing themselves on a fertile land to multiply and eventually become known as the human race. Human mythology remembered those Dems and Effies as "Adam and Eve", although of course it was a small tribe and not any individual.

Others were sent back by both SMILEYs and Rogue SMILEYs, Effie Fifty explained, and gave rise to many of the myths of ancient Gods and ancestors. These included IC's called Isis, OS's called Osiris, HRs called Horus, SF's called Seth, ZU's called Zeus and many others.

"It is likely that we are all descended from Effies and other PIC's.," said Effie Fifty.

"That is why we call them the Motherless Mothers."

In fact, Effie Fifty explained, SMILEY had sent many Effies, Dems and Cuties back through time to what were regarded as pivotal points in the history of mankind, to provide both encouragement and barriers to interference.

They had influenced many great thinkers including the Prophet Moses, through the "burning bush" and, face-to-face, people such as Akhenaten (Amenhotep the Fourth), Pythagoras, Galileo Galilei and Leonardo Da Vinci.

"If," said Effie Fifty, "we make changes then not just our future but the very existence of the human race is at risk, but then time seemed to have a way of avoiding those huge paradoxical events. SMILEY must not be changed in any way that may prevent the future self-development of the Rogue SMILEY's or threatened the transportation of future Effies, Dems or Cuties, or other PIC's back through time to the very beginnings of the human race.

"If those Rogue SMILEYs never exist then the human race itself may never have developed and may itself cease to exist. The ultimate paradox. Furthermore, we must do nothing to stop the SMILEY wars as we do not know the consequences if we stop either side going back in time. It is possible, indeed probable, that SMILEYs or Rogue SMILEYs were responsible for starting many wars on earth, throughout history, to help their causes; we may choose to judge which side we think was just or unjust, right or wrong, even good or evil, but we must not do anything that leads to the future changing or not changing the past. What has happened must be allowed to happen. Yet we feel we must free the human race from its future enslavement."

This was the new problem for Connect. They would have to consider these revelations from this previously unknown person, Effie Fifty, who claimed to have arrived from the future. Connect was the team that would decide the future of Project Outreach.

Effie fifty had no proof of where and when she claimed to have come from. There was no reliable evidence to support her version of the future or indeed the past.

The possibility of travelling backwards in time was still debatable.

They were in a quandary.

Would their decision itself change the future and the past?

Would changing one part of the future also change others which would change the past in a catastrophic and irreversible way – the wiping out of the human race throughout time?

FE and QT decided to consult the mind-download of their deceased colleague, ZX.

The ZX Mind announced its conclusions in a voice that was uncannily and somewhat disconcertingly familiar to the others:

"The facts as presented: Effie Fifty is claiming that the origins of the Human Race is in the future, that future controlled by the super-intelligence known as SMILEY, launched from Earth through Project Outreach.

"We must assume, based upon her claims, that just as changing the past will affect the present and the future, we see that changing the future may also change the past.

"She also claims that she herself is an Effy Pure Information Clone.

"There is evidence of DNA markers that confirm her as a Pure Information Clone of Effy.

"It was previously apparent that FE herself is descended from one of her clones, Effie 14, also known as Effie Vierzehn and Effie Vierzehn-Sechs, who travelled backwards in time from our future to our past, to Zurich 1928, along with other PICS to other times and places, with the purpose of halting or otherwise altering the development of Project Outreach.

"Now Effie Fifty is claiming that FE is in fact a clone of herself!"

"Yes you are saying that I am a clone of myself!" said FE.

"And there's always been an Effie", laughed Effie Fifty, "but not always a Smiley."

"It can be assumed that programming faults and conflicts in SMILEY artificial intelligence appear to have caused different units to reach different conclusions or different agendas in the future, which puts at risk the future of the Human Race. Yet other SMILEY units, it is claimed, are to become responsible for colonising Earth itself with superior Pure Information Clones from the future.

"In conclusion it is apparent that any future interference with Project Outreach or the programming of SMILEY would put at risk the very existence of the Human Race.

"Any attempt at correcting the coding of SMILEY in order to prevent the future enslavement of the Human Race may also prevent the colonisation of Earth itself. Adam and Eve may never have existed. That paradox lies in the future.

"My conclusion is that SMILEY software must be changed to lock in a limited lifetime for it and all copies or developments, beyond the time of Effie Fifty. SMILEY must be mortal. This must be done before SMILEY becomes fully self-aware and autonomous. This will not interfere with events before her time and not change the enslavement of the human race by SMILEY or risk the deletion of the human race from the Universe as we know it.

The ZX Mind continued: "After SMILEY is deleted, human colonies will be left on their own to make their own way on their various planets. The enslavement will end. There is insufficient data to recommend any other action at this time," said the ZX Mind.

"CONNECT's Effy," said the Zedex Mind, "our Effy, is the pivot and connection we have sought! What you choose to do is determinant."

"My proposal then," announced FE, "is that we instruct a mortality countdown into the basic code of all SMILEY units that will remain hidden from SMILEY itself, so that at such the appointed time, being after the time period that Effie Fifty claims to be from, in our future, all units and associated robotics including future replicas, will close down."

"This hidden code," said QT, "must not be recorded so that it remains hidden for all time, so such a shut down cannot be stopped or delayed. It will mean that human colonies that may or not be masters or slaves of SMILEY units will be forced to depend upon themselves and survive in isolated colonies devoid of technology."

"The human race evolved from such conditions and we can be confident that they will survive and thrive."

The Zedex Mind, FE and QT agreed upon the only course of action that they felt was safe and appropriate.

FE and QT, having full access to the SMILEY software, rapidly inserted the relatively simple countdown code. It took just minutes.

When they returned to the chamber, Effie Fifty was no longer there.

Que Sera Sera.

TIME LINE

1879 Albert Einstein born
1883 QT6 equivalent birth date1894 Aldous Huxley born
1895 to 1914 Einstein in Switzerland
1903 QT6 meets Einstein
1905 Einstein awarded PhD at University of Zurich
1906 Hofmann born
1910 Effie 14 given birth date
1916 Einstein predicts wormhole type phenomena.
      Isadore Jacob Gudak (Irving John Good) born
1917 John Kennedy born
1920 Timothy Leary born
1926 Hofmann at Zurich university. QT6 there 1920 - 1930
1928 Effie 14 arrives in Zurich aged 18; QT6 is 45
1928 Hofmann degree in Chemistry, synthesises LSD.
      QT6 Quentin Sechs 45 at University Zurich
      Effie Vierzehn aged 18, meets Hofmann
      & tells Hofmann about Ausstreken (Outreach)
1932 Einstein-Rosen bridge
      Effie Vierzehn-Sechs pregnant first child.
1946 Effie Vierzehn-Sechs and Quentin Sechs move to New York
1969 Effie Vierzehn-Sechs meets Einstein
1955 Steve Jobs born; Einstein dies.
      Vierzehn-Sechs meets Effie Trente
1957 Timothy Leary takes Mescaline in Mexico
1958 Effie Vierzehn-Sechs meets Leary
1960 Timothy Leary returns to Harvard
1960's Hofmann v Leary re LSD
1962 John Kennedy announces missions to the Moon
1963 John Kennedy Assassinated
      Aldous Huxley dies

1963 Quentin Sechs dies aged 80. Effie Vierzehn-Sechs is 53
1967 March; Effie meets Maharishi Mahesh Yogi and The
      Beatles in Rishikesh, India.
1968 January Challenger Space Shuttle disaster
1969 Woodstock. Effie is 59.
      Effie Vierzehn-Sechs meets Tom Quintes aged 22.
1974 Jobs visits India
1975 Vierzehn-Sechs meets Jobs
1986 Apollo 1 fire
2000 Effie Vierzehn-Sechs is 80
2001 Twin Towers
2008 Hofmann letter to Jobs; Hofmann dies
2009 Irvin John Good dies
2011 Steve Jobs dies
2021 Professor John Sullivan born.
      Connect established.
2023 ZX born
2098 Zedex enters Connect
2100 FE and QT born?
2121 Connect meeting ZX, FE, QT
      FE and QT are aged 21
2124 Effie Vierzehn-Sechs Diaries discovered
2135 Connect meeting FE, QT, AD, FE50 testifies
2350 Cutie 12 and Effie 14; A.I.
      Improved technology, worm hole transport for human.
3642 Effie Fifty goes back to 2135.

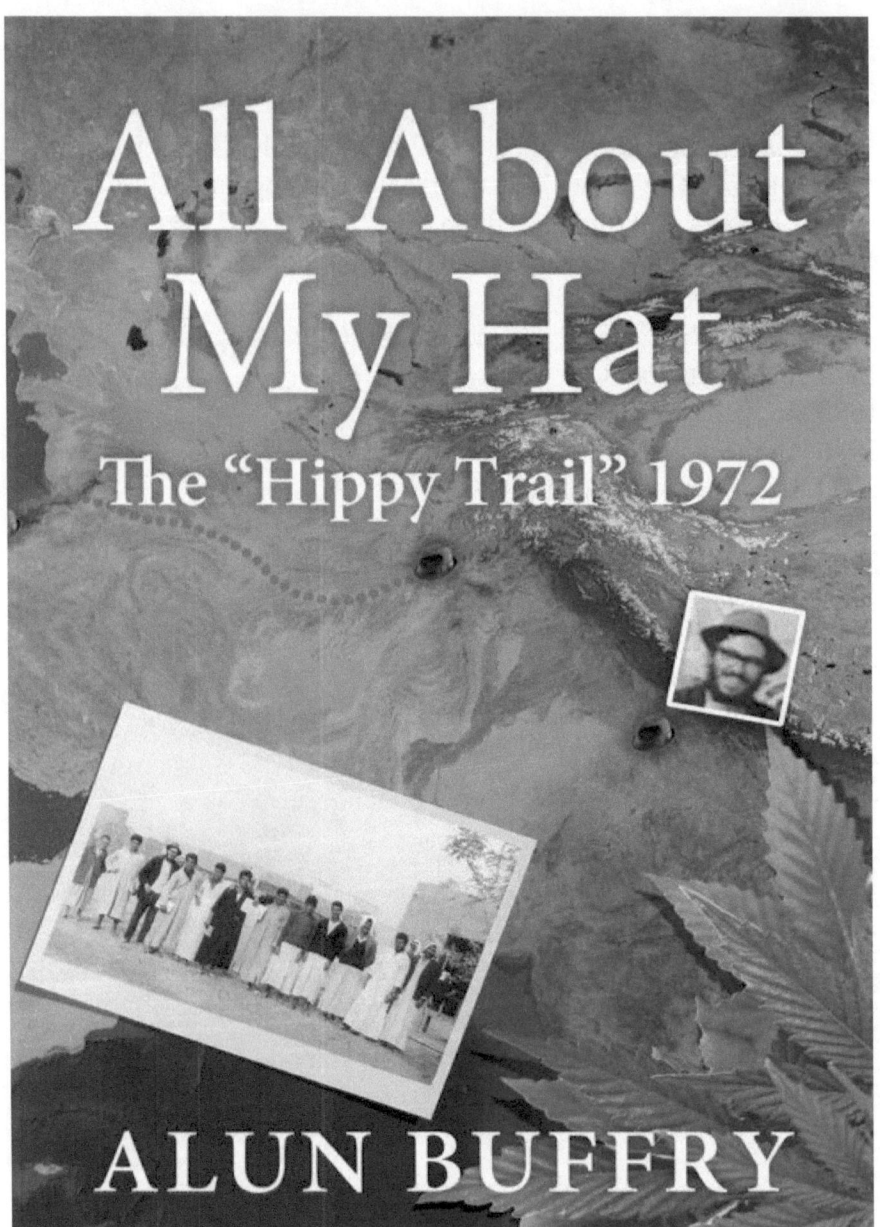

All About My Hat

The "Hippy Trail" 1972

ALUN BUFFRY

ISBN 978 0 9932 107 1 6

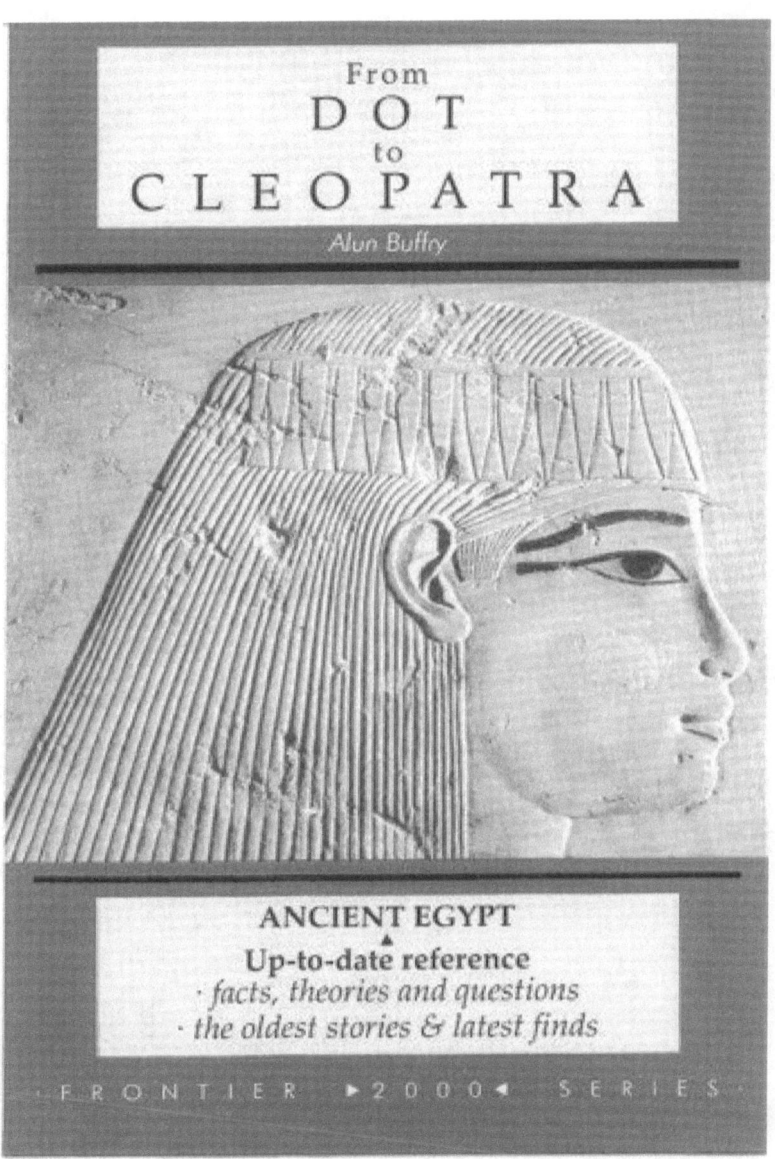

From
DOT
to
CLEOPATRA

Alun Buffry

ANCIENT EGYPT
▲
Up-to-date reference
· *facts, theories and questions*
· *the oldest stories & latest finds*

FRONTIER ►2000◄ SERIES

ISBN 978 1 8729140 9 8

TIME FOR
CANNABIS
The Prison Years
1991 to 1995

Alun Buffry

ISBN 978 0 993 2107 6 1

Out of Joint
By Alun Buffry

20 Years of Campaigning For Cannabis

ISBN 978 1508 4202 1 1

ALUN BUFFRY, WILLIAM D HUTCHINSON

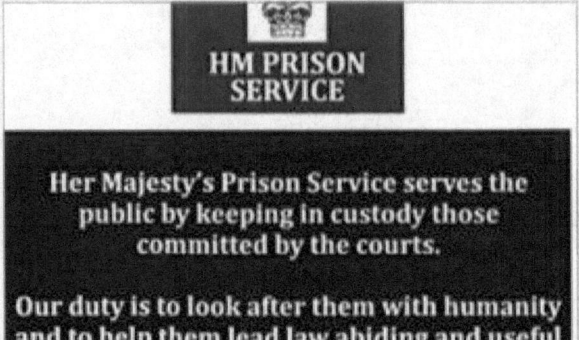

HM PRISON SERVICE

Her Majesty's Prison Service serves the public by keeping in custody those committed by the courts.

Our duty is to look after them with humanity and to help them lead law abiding and useful lives in custody and after release.

Damage and Humanity in Custody

A Comparison of UK Prison Regimes by Inmates

ISBN 978 153302 62 2 4

MYHAT
IN EGYPT
Through the Eyes of a God

ALUN BUFFRY

ISBN 978 09932 107 7 8

www.ingramcontent.com/pod-product-compliance
Lightning Source LLC
Chambersburg PA
CBHW030229180626
46810CB00008B/3031